The King & Elvis

The Day I Become My Idol

Tony Bayliss

Copyright © (2021) Tony Bayliss

All rights reserved. No part of this book may be reproduced, transmitted, or stored in an information retrieval system in any form or by any means, without prior written permission from the author.

This is a work of fiction. Names, characters, places and incidents are products of the author's imagination.

Contents

CHAPTER 1   *5*

CHAPTER 2   *17*

CHAPTER 3   *31*

CHAPTER 4   *42*

CHAPTER 5   *54*

CHAPTER 6   *67*

CHAPTER 7   *79*

CHAPTER 8   *93*

CHAPTER 9   *105*

CHAPTER 10   *116*

CHAPTER 11   *131*

CHAPTER 12   *142*

CHAPTER 13   *156*

CHAPTER 1

There was something about the music blasting through the speakers that soothed Jesse's nerves. Maybe it was because it helped drown out his incessant thoughts. Or because he could scream away his pain and anger as he sang. It was most likely because it was Elvis Presley crooning one of Jesse's favourites, *If I Can Dream*. The song reminded him of everything wrong with his life because it was everything, he wished his life could be, but wasn't.

Jesse swung his head in time with the beats, fingering the buttons on his shirt. He placed a shoe-covered foot on his desk, tapping it as he sang.

"We're lost in a cloud, with too much rain," he swung his hips in time with the words. *"We're trapped in a world that's troubled with pain,"* he echoed *oh troubled with pain* and rushed to continue singing. It was less of singing than screaming, but Jesse still sounded good. He had a voice that was almost as good as Elvis' and, for years, he had done everything as Elvis-like as he could.

"But as long as a man has the strength to dream, he can redeem his soul and fly," Jesse punched his hands into the air, just as the door to his bedroom opened. He turned to see his mom in the doorway, looking just a bit exasperated. Her mouth was forming words, but he couldn't make them out over the loud music

blasting from his speakers, so he gestured for her to hold on, and turned off the speakers. Immediately he did, he wanted to turn them back on; he missed the sound of Elvis.

His mom wasted no time before she started talking again, her voice a little louder than necessary after being in his room with the loud music causing her to shout. "I've been calling you down for dinner for the past five minutes or so."

"Mom–" but she cut him off, as if she knew what he was going to say.

"You need to stop playing your music so loud, Jesse. It's bad for your ears and you know it." She did that thing where she creased her eyebrows and held a hand to her cheek, as if to comfort herself. It was bad for him when she got like this because she looked so worried, like she was a second from tears.

"Mom," he walked to her and gently held her shoulders. He had been taller than her since he turned fifteen. "My ears will be fine. But I was getting to the good part." He eased a smile onto his face and tried to lighten up his eyes. In return, she shook her head at him, not even surprised by his words. "Mom, it's *If I Can Dream*. It's the best of the best. Remember?" He struck a pose, sinking to the floor with his arm stretched over his head, and his right leg stretched out. He hummed the words of the song beneath his breath, all the while smiling at his mom.

She ruffled his hair and cradled his head in her hand. "Please don't play your music so loud again. I want to know if you're okay."

"I am." He wasn't. "I'll be down for dinner soon. Less than five minutes, tops." He took her hand and kissed the inside of her palm.

"Five minutes, Jesse Stockholm." His lips formed a tight smile at hearing his surname – the name he shared with his father – and he watched as she left his room, closing the door behind her. He stood from his pose and shook his legs a little. He made sure to reduce the volume of his speakers a little before he continued playing music.

He let Elvis' voice drown out his thoughts until the maid, Rosetta, knocked on his door, calling him down for dinner once more.

✷✷✷

The story of Jesse Stockholm began with his father, Liam. Liam Stockholm was nothing like his son in his youth. He had always been more inclined towards the Sciences, unlike his son, Jesse, who was obsessed with Elvis Presley and all things that had to do with Rock and Roll in the '50s and '60s; an era long before Liam Stockholm was born.

He was born in the '90s when hippies and their ideologies abound, and he saw himself as unlucky to have been raised by parents who went along with every new age ideology they could find. It was not until he grew older that he discovered the beauty of science and its supposed hand in everything that ever was. A young Liam Stockholm read science textbooks as his parents went to séances.

In high school, he did not bother himself with sports, as he saw it as a waste of time. His parents encouraged him to join activities to "broaden his horizon" but he did none of that, choosing instead to focus on school. Despite their unconventional ways, Liam loved his parents. Most children would have wished for a sibling or two, but Liam wasn't like most children. He knew that having a sibling would have only served as an inconvenience for him, and he always reminded his parents to use contraceptives in order not to give birth to any more children. They barely batted an eye whenever he told them things like that, because theirs was an unconventional family.

Because Liam loved his parents as much as he did, it broke his heart when his father was killed in a car accident. It annoyed him to no extent to see his parents' new age friends at his father's funeral. He was the only one who wore black to the funeral; everyone else wore bright colours, some even wore batiks. They all claimed it was the *soul* of his father. Liam did not care if his father had a colourful soul, he just wanted to bury his father in the way he saw as normal.

He lived alone with his mother for about five months till he went away to Yale on a scholarship. It was there that Liam bloomed. In college, Liam led his class. His professors knew him as a devoted student and scientist. Soon, when he graduated, he got a job as an assistant professor in his department, and he was given grants to fund his research. Barely six years after his father's death, Liam Stockholm became an orphan when his mother committed suicide. Liam readily blamed himself for her death because he had not spoken to her in about two months.

It affected his work and he almost stopped his research, in fact, the university was considering letting him go when Liam encountered what would change his life forever. It was a month after his mother's death, and he had been walking the distance from his research lab to his room when he saw a woman putting up flyers. He slowed down as he watched her, unexplainably entranced. She seemed attractive. She turned to him and gave him an unsure smile. He walked up to her and looked at the flyer without really seeing it. He had been with women before, but he was not an expert at flirting or telling them what they wanted to hear. Usually, he didn't need to do much work because he knew he was handsome.

"Do you listen to them?" The woman had asked him, casting a glance in his direction.

It was then that he *really* looked at the flyer. He had been looking for a distraction, and he had found one. His eyes scanned the list of artists, seeing some unrecognizable names; those were undoubtedly new artistes. What snagged his attention was the mention of old bands which had long since disbanded, and artistes who had either died or stopped singing. Those were the kind of artistes his parents used to listen to.

"Most of the names here don't perform anymore. Some of them haven't even released music in about five decades." She shook his head at his words.

"Yeah, we're just gonna play their music so that whoever's feeling it can dance to it." He couldn't understand why people couldn't just listen to those kinds of music in their homes, but he decided to go because he needed a distraction, and the woman seemed like a good enough one. But the main reason he decided to go was because he wanted to *feel* what his parents felt when they were still alive and listened to songs like *Suspicious Minds* by Elvis Presley.

That was how Liam Stockholm met Lisa Reed. Liam would not have met Lisa again if he had not asked for her number because the bar where the mini-concert held was overcrowded. It was in the bar that he found out how much she loved Elvis Presley. It was in the bar that he sang along to the older songs that he knew, courtesy of his parents. It was in the bar, with tears in his eyes, that he understood, just a little, how music made his parents feel. And after he left the concert with Lisa, he asked her out on a date. And she agreed.

Liam Stockholm found himself again when he returned to work, and he proved himself once more to everyone who knew him. Two years after he met Lisa, they got married. A year after, Jesse Ben Stockholm was born. And that was what Jesse had to live up to.

✵✵✵

The dining table seated six people but only Jesse and his mother were present. His mother had frowned at him when he entered, earning a grimace and a quick apology from him.

"I'm sorry. I'm sorry. I got lost in him." He leaned his head to the side and held his palms together, as if in prayer.

"Just sit down, Jesse." He sat opposite her and cut a slice out of the meatloaf on the tray between them.

"Where's Rosetta?" He waited as she chewed, taking a sip of wine when she swallowed. They were both doing a good job of ignoring the empty chair at the head of the table.

"She went home early. Her daughter isn't feeling too well." He thought about what little he knew about Rosetta and her family. She had two daughters, and she seemed to love her husband. They seemed happy.

"She scolded me a bit when she came to shove me here for dinner. She still sees me as this eight-year-old boy," he shrugged.

"She loves you," his mom stated matter-of-factly.

"I know but I'm an adult. Remember that time I wanted to go for that party? She was all, *Madam Lisa, you can't let this boy go out like this, he's too young*. I'm eighteen, mom. Eighteen." Lisa shook her head and smiled.

"You know how Rosetta is."

"I know how you both are. You could have been sisters." His mom stared into the distance, lost in thought. She seemed to remember herself and glanced to the left, where her husband should have been sitting. Jesse knew what she was thinking; *we couldn't have been sisters. If were, she would have chosen the better husband.*

"I remember when he still came home. It's so long ago." Jesse knew he should not have brought up his dad, but he could not help it.

"Jesse–"

"Why did you marry him?" He looked away from her to ignore the hurt look on her face. "I just want to know, mom. Maybe there's something there that I can't see." Perhaps the worst part about everything to Jesse was how resigned his mom seemed. She used to make up excuses for his dad when he was younger but when he got into high school, he told her not to bother. He knew the kind of man he had for a father. Liam Stockholm was a man more invested in furthering science than he was in keeping his family together. He was never meant to be a father.

"I love Liam." Jesse did not doubt that; what he wanted to know was *why* she loved him. Whenever people found out who his father was, they started swooning over him.

Wow, being his son must be so amazing.

You have such a cool dad.

Your dad is the best dad to have. I wish your dad was my dad.

He just wanted to tell them how wrong they were but all he did was smile at them and walk away. They knew nothing about how much he despised his father for giving himself to everyone and everything *but* his actual family. They knew nothing about how alone Lisa Stockholm felt, raising her child all by herself; she was practically a single mom. They knew nothing about him as a child, desperately wanting his father's attention, and doing everything he could possibly think of to get it – including dressing up and acting like Elvis Presley.

"You love him." He repeated her words at her, trying to understand how, and why.

"You didn't know him before all this. You didn't see him. He didn't–" She stopped herself before she completed her sentence. But Jesse thought he knew what she was going to say. He could fill in the blanks. *He didn't show himself to you. He didn't love you the way he loved me. He didn't care for you.* "What he's giving to the public, to science, that is *him*."

Jesse loved his mother, maybe even more than he loved himself. But, in that second, he hated her for not having made his father choose between them and science. Maybe he would have chosen science and it would have been Lisa and Jesse against the world, or Lisa would have met some other man who would love her the way she deserved, and Jesse would never have been born. And it would have been okay because at least his mother would have been happy.

And if Liam Stockholm had chosen them over science, maybe Jesse would have seen him as others saw him; as this bright, forever-burning light that gives and gives. And maybe Jesse would have loved him. But nothing like that happened.

There were no questions asked when Liam Stockholm chose science and Jesse hated the world for that.

"I guess it's a good thing he isn't around for dinner – or anything, for that matter – because we both know he would have disapproved of my dressing. I think we both know how that would have ended." He tried to sound nonchalant, but he could not perfect it. He was hurt; he always had been. Jesse would have preferred fighting with his dad than having to see him only on the television, and those rare weekends when he came over to the house from work.

He cut another slice of meatloaf and dug into it. "You know what I don't like? How they worship him. We get it, world. Liam Stockholm invented and perfected teleportation. And I think, how much did he do? Those holes in space already made it possible for him to do it, so what exactly did he do?"

Liam Stockholm discovered portholes in space when Jesse was two years old. The science community was aware of the existence of such holes, but they were yet to figure out a way to control it. After years of study, Liam's research discovered a way to harness the fabric of space in such a way that holes could be used to transport a person from one place to another. It was then that fame descended on the Stockholm family, Liam Stockholm in particular.

Although Liam was present in the first two years of Jesse's life, Jesse did not remember. The only piece of evidence for him to brood over was an album of his earlier years. It hurt to look at it because he saw how, over the years, his father gradually extracted himself from their life; from his son's life.

"Jesse." He looked up to find his mom watching him. "One of the things I admired about your dad when I first met him was how dedicated he was to his work. He had this," she waved her hand in the air as she thought of the appropriate word to use. Her face brightened as she found a word. "He had this aura about him when he worked. You should have seen him. He loves his work, and he's good at it. I don't want you discrediting him."

He shook his head at her words, ready to argue with her. "Even before he became my husband, he was my friend. And you won't discredit his work in this house. Just like I won't discredit you for loving and doing what you love." He knew she was talking about his love for Elvis Presley.

"I'll respect your order, mom." She shook her head at him and gave him a sad smile that broke his heart. "Yes, it's an order, and I'll respect it. But I swear, if I find out he's cheating on you, mom."

"Jesse–"

"Please, mom, this, I won't forgive." As far as he knew, his dad was respectful to his mom. "I swear, we're leaving him. You know you're the only reason I'm still here." It was not a complete lie. His mom was his main reason for staying in his parents' house. But he needed to stay for another reason entirely.

"Liam isn't going to do that. If he does, I'll leave him." She looked sad as she said the words, but he did not doubt her. "The first time I met him, he seemed so shy. We both were. I thought he was so handsome, and he wasn't at all like the guys I dated."

"Surprise, surprise," he murmured under his breath, but she heard him and smiled.

"And he was so handsome, he still is. You know you look like him; you've got his eyes and nose." Her voice got softer. "But you have my passion for music." She reached across the table for his hand and took it in hers.

I don't want to leave you, mom. But he remembered what happened on his tenth birthday and he knew it was inevitable.

CHAPTER 2

Jesse watched his mother from across the dining table, his eyes occasionally flicking to the door of the kitchen. He could see Rosetta as she passed the door, hurrying to do some chore in the kitchen. His mom munched on her bacon then checked the time on the relatively antiquated wristwatch she insisted on wearing; as if to be sure they were not behind schedule.

Jesse tapped a beat with his fingers, making sure to time it with the rhythm of the music plugged to his ears through headphones. Lisa Stockholm did not particularly approve of her son blocking everyone out during breakfast but they had agreed that the volume would be low enough that he could hear her – or anyone else, for that matter.

From the corner of his eye, Jesse saw Rosetta walk out of the kitchen. He heard mumbled words so he assumed she greeted his mom. He paused his music and took out his headphones, turning to smile at Rosetta.

"Good morning, Rosetta." She placed a hand on his shoulder, returning his smile. "Breakfast is amazing, as usual. Thanks."

"How was your night, Ben?" He shook his head at her use of his middle name. She was the only one who called him Ben; everyone else called him Jesse.

The only time he'd asked her why she chose to call him by that name, she had responded cheekily, claiming she wanted to have something special of him. He knew Rosetta had always seen him as her son, in some ways, but hearing her tell him that had made him feel special beyond belief. So, he let her call him Ben.

"I have school today. How do you think my night was?" He looked at his mom to see her reaction. She was watching him intently, a smile on her face.

"Good?" Rosetta let out a burst of laughter at his mom's question. They all knew how much Jesse hated school but it wasn't an option for him to be home-schooled. When he was in the sixth grade, his parents decided that he should be home-schooled because of how different he was from the other kids at school. He got bullied almost every day because of his love for Elvis Presley, and his decision to dress and act like him.

Liam Stockholm hired a tutor for Jesse but the lessons did not last long; the woman could not handle Jesse's sporadic, atypical behaviour. She quit after two weeks. Jesse later begged his parents to re-enrol him into school; he wanted to be around people his age. And that was that about home schooling for Jesse Stockholm.

"It'll get better. And if it doesn't, you're graduating soon." He looked back at Rosetta whose face had sobered up quickly.

"I think college would be better, Jesse." He shook his head at his mom. He didn't plan on going to college, but she didn't need to know that yet. If he was being honest with himself, he suspected his mom already knew about his plans to skip college – but she didn't know why.

"*I* know it won't." His mom checked her wristwatch again and sighed.

"Thanks for breakfast, Rosetta," she said as she pushed her chair away from the table, creating room for her to stand.

Jesse took that as his cue to get up and quickly scarfed down what remained of his breakfast. He hugged Rosetta and walked to the living room to get his bag.

✱✱✱

Jesse connected his phone to his mom's car, and pressed play on Elvis Presley's *Suspicious Minds*. For as longs as he could remember, it had been a tradition of theirs to play old songs whenever they were in a car; no matter how short the trip was. Their music playing leaned more toward Elvis' songs when Jesse decided Elvis was the best musician that ever was.

"I don't want it too loud. Maybe you should reduce the volume a bit." He glanced at his mom as she spoke, her fingers tightening around the wheel.

"Sure," his finger was already on the button to reduce the volume. When the music was not as loud as before, he turned to her and asked, "How about now? Is this okay?"

"Yeah, it's alright like this." His mom nodded along to the music, her fingers tapping a rhythm against the wheel.

"*Why can't you see what you're doing to me,*" he turned to his mom, waiting for her to complete the lyrics.

She did not disappoint him.

"*When you don't believe a word I say?*" They smiled at each other, getting into the music.

They both rushed to sing the chorus. "*We can't go on together with suspicious minds,*" he echoed *suspicious minds* with a smile on his face. It did not escape his notice how good they sounded together. Jesse knew he had an amazing voice. He assumed he got it from his mom who was an even more amazing singer. She had a clear tenor voice that Jesse was jealous of. "*And we can't build our dreams on suspicious minds.*"

✸✸✸

"Stockholm." Jesse was intent on ignoring the boy behind him. "Stockholm!" But apparently, the boy did not want him to. He turned to see Aaron Harrison. As usual, he was flanked on each side of the lunch table by two of his friends. Jesse never bothered to remember their names.

"What do you want, Harrison?" For some reason or the other, they always chose to address each other by their last names. Maybe it was supposed to be a macho thing.

"Halloween's over, you know?" The worst part about Harrison was how intelligent he was. Despite the stupidity and senselessness of bickering with him to the point where it bordered on obsession, and bullying – at least on Harrison's end –

he was still a smart guy. "You can ditch the Elvis Presley costume."

That earned a laugh from people around them. For the life of him, he could not understand why it still amused them; it had been about four years since he wore regular clothes to school.

"I don't think he can, Aaron. I think the costume's melded to his body." The quip came from one of the guys on Aaron's table.

"And I guess you want to see my body." The boy at the receiving end of his words blushed scarlet. Everyone knew he was into broad shoulders, and rough faces, rather than curves and wide hips; but he had not officially come out. Jesse did not have it in him to feel guilty for outing him. Although the thought of his mom finding out that he did, the disappointment that was sure to be in her eyes, it made him remorseful for a second or two.

"Even if he wanted to, which he doesn't," Harrison cast a glance at the people around them as if to intimidate them into silence, "you've gotta dress like a normal person, Stockholm."

Jesse had never liked Harrison because he was everything his own father wished he was. It didn't help that their fathers worked together. Besides, everyone knew not to trust people with a first name as their last names. His dislike for Harrison bordered on a hatred that simmered, like it was waiting for something to make it explode.

Jesse did not know that the final ingredient to make his dislike explode into a full-blown hatred was just around the corner.

"I'd say go fuck yourself but you've already done that one too many times. It shows, Harrison." He gave Harrison a scowl and turned away from him. He could see the furtive glances the few people on his table cast at him, but he ignored them.

"You know," he could hear how agitated Harrison was getting. People like him couldn't stand *not* being in the spotlight. "It's no wonder your dad is only your dad when he has to do press releases. I'd also be ashamed if I had a son like you."

Jesse almost laughed. Harrison's words weren't anything he hadn't said to himself over the years, so he ignored him. It was no big deal; he was already used to it.

"I guess you don't know how much of a freak you look like. And Elvis Presley? Of all people. He's been dead for so long, man. You might as well be dead. Besides–"

He knew what Harrison wanted to say so he stopped him before he could go too far. He could take being insulted to an inch of his life. He could accept insults regarding his family. What he could not, and would not, accept were insults directed at Elvis Presley, or his love for him.

"I'll stop you right there." He stood from his seat and faced Harrison's table. "You don't insult or slander Elvis Presley."

Harrison scoffed and stood, coming round his table to stand in front of Jesse. The two boys were nearly the same height, but Harrison was taller by an inch.

"And if I do?" Harrison cocked his head to the left and folded his arms across his chest in what Jesse assumed to be an intimidating stance.

"Just don't." He mirrored Harrison's stance, as if to say *you don't scare me.*

Harrison stepped closer to him, crowding his personal space. Jesse didn't budge. "Elvis Presley is a dead man, and I bet you jerk off thinking of him, even though his music is absolute crap."

Even though Harrison was right in front of him, he spoke loud enough for the entire cafeteria to hear.

It was safe to say no one expected it when Harrison bent over in pain, his hands clutched over his crotch area. The shriek he released from his lips drew everyone's attention fully. Before anyone could intervene, Jesse yanked Harrison to his full height and held him by the shoulder. He managed to sock him in the jaw before he was yanked away by a random guy.

A glance at Harrison's table showed his friends frozen and wide-eyed, watching as everything unfolded before them. He shifted his attention once more to Harrison who was being held up by another guy. Jesse had seen him around in school; they were in the same music class.

Harrison was struggling against the guy's muscular arms. Jesse shoved against the person holding him, and kicked Harrison's stomach. The guy holding Harrison – James, that was his name – loosened his hold, and Harrison took the opportunity to return the favour by punching his stomach. Jesse feared he could have burst an internal organ; that was how painful it was.

"Both of you! Mr Stockholm and Mr Harrison!" It was then that Jesse noticed the chaos around him. Some people must have alerted the school authorities because his History teacher, Mr Swain, stood to the side with school security.

The hands holding him loosened their grip. Jesse's heart was beating a mile a minute but, somehow, all he felt was calm. His heart and mind were not in agreement.

"You will both follow me to the Principal's office, and these security officers will accompany us to be sure that you don't run off." Mr Swain nodded at the security officer who stepped forward. Jesse didn't need to be told twice.

The entire walk to the Principal's office, students in the hallway kept gawking at them. Some of them must have been in the cafeteria because he heard whispers discussing what happened between him and Harrison.

He's such a freak.

He deserved it. What kind of freak show dresses like Elvis Presley? The dude's been dead for decades.

I still can't believe he's Liam Stockholm's son.

You should have heard Harrison's scream. I'm almost a hundred percent sure he wet himself.

The last one made him smirk. It was good to know he wasn't the only one who harboured animosity toward Harrison.

Finally, they arrived at the Principal's office and were instructed to wait outside. Mr Swain was allowed to see the Principal after he explained the situation to the Principal's secretary.

The only thing stopping him from continuing the fight with Harrison was the lone security officer standing to the side. She was very beautiful but her stance, and facial expression, told him to watch himself around her. He was somewhat relieved when the secretary instructed them to go into the Principal's office.

He gave Harrison a wide enough berth before entering after him. It took all of his self-control not to say anything to him.

He could feel the intense gaze of Mr Swain and Principal Harley on him so he quickly took a seat on the chair opposite the Principal, doing his best to ignore Harrison who was on the chair beside him.

"Mr Swain has already told me his account of things, but I want to know yours. Of course, the security cameras captured everything." Principal Harley gave a seemingly nonchalant shrug. Jesse got the unspoken message: "If you lie, it's at your expense. I already know the truth, and even if I didn't, I'll find out."

For about thirty seconds, neither he nor Harrison spoke. A glance at Principal Harley showed how unnerved he was, in contrast with Mr Swain who looked about a second from losing his cool.

"Harrison insulted me, even after I warned him not to. I take the blame for hitting him first but, in my defence, he offended me and mine." He squared his jaw and resisted the urge to glance at Harrison. The tension in the office was so taut, he could feel Harrison's annoyance.

Principal Harley looked at Harrison, clearly awaiting his own explanation. Jesse kept his ears peeled for lies in Harrison's account. He had been expecting it but when Principal Harley told them he was going to inform their parents, Jesse found that his heart beat double time. All he could think of was how his mom would react to the news.

She's going to be so disappointed.

"We're going to give you this report to give your parents. It contains your escapades in details. If your parents want to get in touch with me regarding your suspension, my work number is in the report."

I can't believe I let myself get suspended. For three weeks!

Finally dismissed, and with his report in hand, Jesse stood from his chair and hurried to the door of Principal Harley's office. Before he could leave, the Principal's voice stopped him.

"And just in case you decide to be smart, you should know we're going to call your parents." With those words still ringing in his ears, he hurried through the empty hallways, not even bothering to stop by his locker before he left school. The permit with the Principal's signature ensured no one questioned his leaving school before it ended.

✳✳✳

Jesse was sure he was making a hole in the floor with all the pacing he was doing. Not that he could help it. His mom was going to be home soon, and she was undoubtedly going to talk to him about his suspension.

It was then that it occurred to him. The school would have called his dad, too. His heart was racing a mile a minute at seeing his dad. He had no illusions as to the confrontation that would happen between them. Although he didn't much care for his dad, it always irked him how audacious he was. He was near absent in Jesse's life but situations like the one in school had him running home.

It was ironic because Jesse knew his dad didn't see the house he and his mom lived in as home. He had an apartment closer to his lab – that was where he spent his nights, when he decided to sleep. The world, including Jesse, knew Liam

Stockholm's real home was his lab. Everyone knew his wife was Science, and his child was his teleportation machine.

A knock on his door startled him and brought him out of his thoughts. Rosetta looked pityingly at him. He had already told her everything that happened.

"Mom's home?" He rubbed at his shoulder.

"And your dad." He had expected it but hearing her say it…

He followed her downstairs. He barely even thought of how he had not heard either of their cars. At the bottom of the stairs, he could hear them. His father was this close to shouting, and he already knew his mom would be trying her best to stop herself from shouting back at him.

"If you hadn't encouraged him, Lisa. That's all I'm saying!" Jesse hated the way his dad sounded. He was always so academic, and serious.

"That's what he's passionate about, Liam. And you can't blame me for raising our son in the way I saw fit. Sometimes I think you forget, you know?" He heard how hysterical his mom was getting and he hurried to the living room, leaving Rosetta by the stairs.

"You think I forget? I admit I wasn't around but I'm doing what I see as right by you and him."

"So, you see abandoning your wife and son for science as right? You see choosing the *world* over us as the best fucking decision you've ever made in your entire fucking miserable life?" Jesse stood at the edge of the living room, watching the man he called his father with equal measure of hate and love. He hated that even after everything, he still wanted to have a connection with him. He hated how he could see himself in him; in his height, his eyebrows, his jaw.

Both his parents looked positively scandalised by his words, his dad especially. His dad turned to his mom, ready to chastise her once more – but Jesse stopped him.

"I don't want you saying anything to her." It was then that his father *finally* looked at him. Jesse walked into the living room and stood by his mom. "She was there for me when I needed her. You weren't. And if anyone should be chastised, it's you. But no one says anything because as much as we all love to claim that society has moved forward, people don't see anything wrong with a man abandoning his family."

"Jesse–" his mom started but he cut her short.

"No, mom. We can have the discussion about how I got myself suspended but he doesn't deserve to be here for that." He took a step closer to his dad. "You will not disrespect her. Not while I'm here. Not while I'm alive."

It was Liam Stockholm's laughter that broke the silence that descended in the living room after Jesse spoke. Jesse and his mom looked at him, stoic expressions on their faces.

"Do you remember what I told you on your tenth birthday? I bet you thought I hated you, by telling you that. But it's the truth." Jesse watched as his father spoke, the words hitting him even as the memory took him.

You could never be Elvis.

CHAPTER 3

Jesse still remembered his tenth birthday like it was yesterday. Even though he did not really have friends, his mom had invited other kids from his Elementary school, especially those from his class. He had begged his mom to make it a costume party because he knew most kids his age would want to come if they got to dress up.

Back then, he had made it no secret how much he wanted his dad in his life. The days leading up to his birthday had seen him asking his mom, every moment he could, whether or not his dad would show up at his birthday party. It had nothing to do with his schoolmates, and most of their parents, wanting to meet his dad, and everything to do with the man who contributed to his birth being present at his birthday.

The day came, and everyone who was invited was around. Liam Stockholm was nowhere to be seen. Jesse had already started hearing some of the other kids murmur about how his dad wasn't going to be around for his birthday. They felt bad for him. He didn't want anyone feeling sorry for him; he already did that enough for two people. His mom had had to persuade him to do the performance he had been practicing. He hadn't said it then but she had known – it was for his dad. He was halfway done with his presentation when his dad arrived. He had barely contained his urge to run to him, choosing instead to finish his performance.

That night, after everyone had left, and only him and his parents remained, his dad broke his heart. He had run to meet him, and showed him his costume. His dad had simply turned to his mom and asked her why he was dressed the way he was. The details of their argument are now murky in Jesse's mind, but he remembered that he had pushed his dad away from his mom. He had wanted them to take a break from their argument and look at *him*.

The words his father spat at him before he walked away would forever ring in his head. *You could never be Elvis.*

And as Jesse watched as his father walked away, his face twisted up in scorn and hate, he couldn't fathom how a father would ruin his child in the way his did. Eight years later, and they still came back to the same thing. It didn't matter that they could have been mistaken for brothers. Jesse walked to his mom and hugged her, drawing strength from her as much as she was from him.

"Are we still going to talk about my suspension?" He uttered the words, more to lighten the mood than anything. But he didn't want to talk about his suspension, he wanted to spend the next few days with her. Before he left, he wanted to memorise everything about her.

She pulled back and ruffled his hair. Laughing, she said, "we're gonna have to talk about that one, mister."

And even as he laughed with her, he saw the sadness in her eyes, and he knew they were both pretending to be what they weren't – at least in that moment. And Jesse realised that as much as he loved her, he had to find his own way. He had to prove his father wrong.

✲✲✲

Over the next few days, Jesse spent as much time as he could with his mom. Whatever time he couldn't spend with her was spent with Rosetta. He gave himself a week with them. Every night, as he lay on his bed, he told himself: *it's only a week, Jesse. I swear, if you spend more than a week…*

He couldn't finish the empty threats to himself. All he could think of was how miserable he would be if he stayed; if he didn't leave to do what needed to be done. All the while, he had been saving money in his room, in one of his old shoeboxes. He made sure to keep it high up where even Rosetta couldn't reach. It helped that he had started saving months before he decided to leave.

He had also been withdrawing as little money as he could without drawing attention to himself, so he had over three thousand dollars in cash. He thought it was enough for what he needed to do. He had already done his research in internet cafes; he didn't want anyone to track him down.

Finally, the eve before the day he decided to leave home came and he was feeling sentimental. His mom must have noticed something off about him because she practically shoved him to the theatre room, and she let him pick the movie.

Less than five minutes into the movie, she turned to him with a slight frown on her face. "Are you okay? You've been a little off for some time now." She considered him thoughtfully for about a minute – throughout which he was scared she would see his true intentions written across his forehead – and her frown deepened further. "It's not because of your suspension, is it? You know I believe you when you say you're going to do better."

He shrugged it off, wanting to get the attention off him, and onto the action movie they were supposed to be watching, but weren't.

"I don't know. I've just… I guess it's one of those days, you know?" He wondered if she was thinking of how tightly he had hugged Rosetta before she left.

She offered him a sad smile that told her she knew. And when she pulled him in for a hug – albeit an awkward one, all thanks to the seats in the home theatre – he didn't resist.

Later, at night, he let the tears roll down his cheeks. He wiped angrily at them. He wasn't even sure if time travel was real. *If teleportation is real, how far off can time travel be?* He knew the voice in his head wasn't far from right. He had read about different studies and findings on the subject of time travel, and he knew there were different views on the possibility of its applicability. Even without research, Jesse knew that scientists such as his dad – scientists, *especially* his dad – were sceptical of the effects of time travel. But Jesse dismissed them as being too sceptical. His view was that everything had a bad side, some more than others.

That thought was what pushed him off his bed, careful to keep his steps light. The last thing he wanted to do was wake his mom up in the middle of the night, and have her asking why there were dried tears on his cheeks – or even why he was up so late. *It's best to avoid questions of any kind.*

He went to his desk, and picked a notebook. He was about to tear a page from it when he realised it was one of the gifts Rosetta gave him on his eighteenth birthday. He could still smell the wafts of tomatoes that came from the kitchen as she prepared lasagne specially for him. Of course, he had shared it with her and his mom.

Cursing himself, Jesse placed the notebook to the side. He resolved that he was going to take it with him, along with his picture of Rosetta. He would keep the things he had of her with him, till he could come back.

He picked a random notebook he had probably gotten from school – judging by the unnecessarily large school logo on the cover – and tore a page from it. He began drafting a note in his head. *Dear mom, please forgive me for being a coward.*

"You've been a fucking coward your whole life." Startled by how loud his voice was in the silence of the dark, he lightly smacked his forehead.

He thought of how much he loved her. She had been there for him his whole life, and, in a twisted way, he was doing this for her. He wanted so desperately to prove his father wrong. For every time he had talked down at his mom, for every time he had blamed her for teaching Jesse to love. For all those times, and many more, Jesse wanted to show him that he could be Elvis, and he was going to be Elvis.

So, he put his hand against the paper and wrote his heart to his mom. In the same paper, he apologised to her, promising to be back as soon as he could. He gave her permission in the form of his signature to use the money left in his account for herself, and for Rosetta. He knew his mom would give everything to Rosetta. She would claim Rosetta needed it more, and just the thought of that made him smile. His smile was a wobbly, weak thing.

He tore another page from the notebook, and wrote to Rosetta. He told her to look after his mom, and he told her how much he appreciated and loved her. He also promised to be back if he could, but some part of him thought it was a wasted promise. By morning, Jesse Stockholm was a thousand miles from home.

✱✱✱

The young man that was crossing the busy German street, long legs encased in a pair of well-worn cargo pants, would not be recognisable to anyone that knew him some fifteen months before. He had shaved all of his facial hair, leaving only a small goatee that he thought suited him quite well – but that only said loads about his sense of style, as goatees had long since been out of fashion. What his mom had, once upon a time, fondly called his 'Elvis Presley sideburns' had long since been carefully shaved off. He had replaced his 70s style clothing for more modern clothes, all in the name of blending in.

Jesse quickened his steps the closer he got to his apartment. It was a tiny thing that cost less money than he had at first assumed it would. He had paid an advance of two months' rent, his plan to stay in Europe made easier by the fluidity of European borders – at least for those still members of what remained of the European Union.

He quickly unlocked his door, subtly checking his surroundings to make sure no one had followed him. He kicked off his boots, sighing as his knees hit the inflatable mattress he had called a bed for the past six months, give or take.

It was always a stressful day for him whenever he called his mom. He didn't even know why he had called her; they had spoken days before. But sometimes, he needed to hear her voice, and just feel how much he missed her. He had spoken with her for a bit, before she passed the phone to Rosetta who had spoken Italian with him just for the sake of it. Rosetta had passed the phone back to his mom who had asked when he was returning home. The question had made his throat tight, and he had had to swallow down the groan of frustration that threatened to spill from his throat.

It was as if his mom didn't care how many months he had been gone – he knew she didn't – because every time they spoke, she asked him when he was coming home. And it *killed* him to hear how absolutely broken she sounded. He had told her the same thing he always did whenever she asked him: *as soon as I can, mom. I promise.* And Jesse was the worst human in existence because he had been promising for fifteen months.

After the call with his mom, he had messaged one of his contacts, the one who finally had the information he needed. Jesse could hardly believe it; after years, he had finally met the man who could change everything for him. He had sent about three hundred dollars to his contact as payment for the information – but that was after he had checked out the address given to him. It was supposedly for a government-owned building industry that had been shut down years ago. Jesse was almost breathless when he saw that it was in the same city as he was.

Jesse had taken a train to the area, and he had walked the remaining way to the building. He had ducked behind buildings, in case someone – anyone – was watching. When he got to the rear entrance of the building, like he had been advised to, he knocked. At first, he was scared his knock would attract attention because of how loud it sounded in the night, but it didn't. So, he knocked again, and when there was no answer, he slipped a paper beneath the door like his contact had advised him to. Before long, the door opened but the darkness behind him, and inside the building, didn't illuminate the man's face. The man examined his face, and he must have been satisfied with what he saw because he let Jesse into the building.

He followed the man blindly, almost stepping on a cat, when the man tossed over his shoulder, "be careful where you step."

And that was the only warning he was given. He followed the man belowground, if the slightly reduced temperature was anything to go by. The basement was lit brighter than above-ground, and Jesse was glad he wasn't claustrophobic because he couldn't have been able to stand the thought of being totally underground.

He looked around the space, wondering how the air was kept clean.

"There's something of an air filterer. I made it myself." Jesse turned to the man who was watching him intently. He recognised the face, as he had seen it many times online.

"Elias Abendroth." He would recognise the pessimistic arch of his eyebrows wherever he saw it. That arch that was in contrast to his viewpoint as a scientist; ever-optimistic, and ready to explore new things.

"You are a spitting image of your father, Jesse Stockholm. And I didn't even need to read the paper to know your identity." His voice made his intonations and pronunciations sound more serious. "Or should I address you in English?" He switched to English, his voice only losing some of its weightiness.

Jesse shook his head, about to cross his arms but hastily deciding against it. If he was to believe articles he had read on the man in front of him, he was sure to see it as a nervous, or defensive stance. And although Jesse was nervous, it was only in part due to finally being a step closer to time travel. "I'm fluent in German."

"Okay, then!" Elias clapped his hands together, startling Jesse only a little bit. The sound resonated around the room, and Jesse's concern must have shown on his face because Elias was quick to ease his worries. "Don't worry. No one can hear us from so far below, and even if they could, the walls and doors are soundproof."

Jesse followed him even deeper into the room, knowing he should be a bit terrified, but only feeling his anxiety pile up inside him. He could feel its fingers caressing his brain with feather-light touches. He distracted himself by observing the room he was in.

Every corner was as organized as could be. Jesse always thought scientists were a messy bunch, his dad included, but Elias Abendroth's lab was even more organized than Rosetta. His gaze was soon transfixed on an oval-shaped contraption. It seemed like a door of some sorts, like something a person could walk through, except there was no *door* – and it was oval-shaped. Jesse would not have assumed it was the time machine if he hadn't seen how Elias' expression had become of adoration.

Elias stopped a few feet from it, and Jesse stopped just beside him. It was then that he noticed the small computer-like system attached to the time machine. It was one of his father's newer models that facilitated teleportation. Somehow, Elias had manipulated it to create time travel. Jesse had never respected anyone like he did Elias in his life; at least in that moment.

"I'd ask you to explain the science to me, but that would take precious time that I don't have." Jesse glanced at Elias and saw that the man remained still, his gaze fixed on the time machine. He was clearly lost in thought.

After a few minutes of silence, Jesse finally spoke. He had a feeling Elias knew what he wanted but he was going to have him say it. Maybe he just wanted the opportunity to say no to Jesse's request.

"I'll just start by saying that I have money. And I'm willing to use it to help you do more research." A glance at Elias showed him still fixated on the time machine, but this time, with a puzzle look on his face. "I know you don't have much funds for your research, and you need to be able to make your invention fool proof in order to get the support of the government, and the scientific community. If you help me with this, I'll give you money."

Finally, Elias turned to him. "You don't understand, Jesse Stockholm. I have only figured out how to go to the time. I'm yet to figure out how to bring back to *this* time."

CHAPTER 4

"I was happy when I made some strides in altering teleportation, by using a wormhole that I was able to–" Elias Abendroth paused and looked at Jesse. "I won't bore you with the scientific details, which is not to say that you won't understand them."

"I am aware of your works, and theories, Mr. Abendroth. There's no need to explain to me." Jesse could see that the man was shaking with excitement. He could even imagine that Abendroth had not talked to enough people about his invention.

"Elias will do, I think. You must know how unstable wormholes are. I have been able to harness them long enough to let a time traveller walk through, and into their desired time, but I haven't been to stabilise them long enough to find an exit. That is, to put it simply, I'm yet to find the door that leads back to our present. I said *our* because–"

"Time, as well as space, is relative, and our present is not another's present." Jesse finished Abendroth's sentence. He had not lied when he said he was familiar with the man's works and theories.

"Exactly. Another glitch, you could call it, that I am working toward fixing is where in time the time traveller can go. As you must be well aware of, seeing as your father pioneered its invention, teleportation technology simply brings together two locations in space, allowing for seamless movement from one location to another." Abendroth had gestured to his time machine, and continued. "My time machine brings two points in time together, and it uses some elements of teleportation technology to bring together two points in space."

Jesse had been listening intently, and he could see where Abendroth was headed. He knew there was a 'but' ahead, and he needed to know what it was. "What's the catch?" He switched to English, allowing him to properly phrase the question.

"The *catch*, Jesse Stockholm, aside from the inability to return to your present?" Elias Abendroth spoke in English, his accent catching as he emphasised the word. "Travel to a particular time may be done, but it is only as long as that time frame is already in existence."

"The past." Jesse had whispered to himself, but Abendroth must have heard him because he nodded in agreement.

"Yes, Jesse, the past. Considering these factors, it is highly advised that you don't continue with this plan of yours, whatever it may be."

But Jesse's mind was as far from the room as it could be. His thoughts were on a house all the way across the world, with a woman inside. A woman who had been expecting her son to return home for more than a year now. His mom: Lisa Stockholm. He couldn't leave her, especially when he had promised her over and over that he would return home. What kind of a dick would he be if he didn't? Just the thought of never seeing her again sent his heart into a flurry of panic.

Jesse had felt a hand on his shoulder and his head cleared enough for him to see Abendroth's face creased in concern.

"Maybe you should sit down, Jesse. To avoid any… unfortunate event from happening." Abendroth pulled a chair from the corner of the room and placed it beside Jesse, who lowered himself unto it. Jesse sat, staring into the distance. It was the first time he found himself doubting his plan, his decisions.

I've spent two years planning this and it's all a waste.

"Maybe if you," Jesse began, looking up at Elias Abendroth, "maybe I can wait for you to find out what you can. If you ask others for help, I'm sure they will have some sort of solution." He knew how frantic he sounded, but this was his life.

"Even if I were to wait, it might take months, years. And there is no guarantee that I'll find a 'solution', as you put it." But Jesse could hear the excitement in Abendroth's voice. The man was a scientist, of course he was excited by the possibility of breakthrough in his research. If not for anything, Jesse had him because of that.

"I'll wait. I'll give you time to find whatever needs finding, Abendroth, but I can only wait so long." Jesse tried to steel his voice, but he was panicking. "I'll return tomorrow, and we can discuss much more."

But all Abendroth had done was look at him with the most intense look Jesse had ever been given. Finally, he had said, in the gravest of tones, "there are dangers tied to this route, Jesse Stockholm. You have your whole life ahead of you."

But Jesse was having none of it. He stood abruptly, causing the chair to topple backwards. He turned to pick it, and righted it. "Sorry about that," he apologised to Abendroth who simply shook his head.

"You are quite different, Jesse Stockholm. Sometimes, that may not be the best thing." With the look Abendroth had casted his way, Jesse wondered if the man knew his reason behind his desire to time travel.

Jesse had hovered for a few seconds, feeling awkward. "Well, goodbye." He had spoken in English, waving and nodding at Abendroth. "I'll be here tomorrow, if I can."

"Goodbye, then." Jesse had taken a good look at the makeshift lab, before turning on his heel. He had made his way out of the building, not the least bit surprised when the door clicked behind him, signifying that it had locked itself.

And as Jesse lay on the bed in the little room, he refused to call his, he thought of all that had been revealed to him, and sighed. Tomorrow, he would return to Abendroth's lab, and if all went well, within a few months, he would be years into the past.

✳

Jesse woke up as early as six the next morning. It was not that he had to be at Abendroth's lab that early, it was merely a force of his nature. In the days following the morning that he ran away from home; Jesse had feared that people had been sent to bring him back. Every step he took was miles away from home. It was stupid of him to have thought of that, but he had wanted to believe it.

In reality, the only person who could have sent people to look for him was his mom, and he knew she did not have the money to do that, knowing that he could be anywhere in the world. Jesse knew that if his dad had sent people to get him, he would have followed them without a thought. It annoyed him to no end, but it was the truth.

He had lost whatever hope he had in his father when he saw an interview his father had with the press. He had just left his car and was walking to his lab when the press accosted him. It had struck Jesse then, how much he did not know his father. He did not even know if the man hated being questioned by the press. Judging by the slight scowl that he quickly covered up with the fakest of smiles, Jesse thought he did. From what little he knew of Liam Stockholm; the man saw things that did not help his research as a waste of his oh-so-valuable time. And there was no way that a reporter asking him questions about his thoughts on the dangers of smoking was useful to him.

Jesse's attention had moved away from the interview until the mention of 'son' snagged it. He had whipped his head to the TV so fast; it was a wonder he did not have whiplash.

"We have reports that your son hasn't been seen in school, and he wasn't present for his graduation?" The reporter had hurried after his father, and Jesse could not help but feel bad for the reporter.

"My son–" Liam began, but he was interrupted by the reporter.

"Jesse Stockholm." The reporter nodded at the camera as if to make sure the viewers knew who Liam Stockholm's son was.

His father's tightened lips were the only indication that he was irked. "Jesse is nineteen years old. He's a man. He decided to leave Lisa and I, and we respect his decision."

Jesse had felt his eyes pool with tears, which he rapidly blinked away. His dad had some nerve, turning it all on him like he had been the one to abandon his family.

But you are like him. Jesse had tried his best to ignore the voice in his head, but it had continued. *You left your mom, and she's your family.*

He had quickly left the diner, making sure to put his head down. But that was months ago when he had just left home.

That doesn't make it any easier to remember. Jesse took a quick shower and brushed his teeth. He dusted out his cargos from the day before and wore it. Doing laundry was not his favorite thing, even though his building had a laundry room. He did his best to minimize interaction with other people unless it was necessary. He did not need more people to leave behind when he finally left – because he *was* going to leave.

He picked his backpack, which had everything important to him, and left his room, but not before making sure he had locked it properly. He kept his head down all the way to the diner he had chosen to eat at that day. Jesse always tried to have a wide enough selection of places to eat; he did not want anyone to notice him for whatever reason. He walked as briskly as he could to a diner that he knew was several streets over. It helped that he had never been there before.

Inside, he ordered his breakfast in German, and he cracked a joke or two with the waitress. Jesse knew it was better to blend in and be as inconspicuous as possible. He even watched the news, commenting on it when the waitress came with his bill.

Having eaten, Jesse made his way to the subway and took a train to the industrial area of the city. It was day, so he knew he might look a bit suspicious to some, a guy with a black backpack and a neck so focused on the ground that it suggested he did not want to be noticed or approached. Hopefully, he would remain left alone till he reached Abendroth's lab.

But Jesse was careful. Even with his attention seemingly on the ground, he was fully aware of his surroundings. It was a skill he had mastered out of necessity, more than anything else.

Finally, Jesse stood in front of the back door of the building. He knocked and waited, but he did not hear movement from the other side of the door. He was about to knock again when the door opened. He quickly stepped inside, but not before closing the door behind him. Abendroth did not speak a word;

he simply walked down the same corridors that he had walked yesterday, and Jesse followed him. He was careful with his step, even though he could barely see where he was going.

"You're terribly early today." Jesse was spooked out for about a second till he realized it was only Abendroth talking.

"I think," his voice sounded extra loud in the dark, so he softened his tone. "Considering the fact that I came here last night, some minutes past seven in the morning isn't too early."

Abendroth hummed, whether in agreement, Jesse did not know. "I will need some funds to continue with the research, as you well know."

"Yes, of course!" Jesse's eyes adjusted to the bright lights of the lab, and he blinked rapidly. "The contrast between the dark and the light is a bit too… contrasting, in my opinion."

"Oh, I know. Life would not give you any notice that things are about to go awry; neither would my lab."

Jesse saw faults in the man's logic, but he decided against arguing. "How much would you need, exactly?"

"I would prefer to get the money in installments. I had something of a gambling problem in my youth, but my love for science won me over." Jesse was sure his shock was evident on his face. It had less to with Abendroth's supposed gambling problem, and more to do with the ease with which the man mentioned it. His father would never talk about something like that, especially with someone he barely knew, and would surely see to be just a boy.

"Whichever is more convenient for you, Elias." Jesse set down his backpack, making sure to keep a grip on it with his right hand. With his left hand, he unzipped it and pulled out a few bills from the hidden layer of the backpack. He counted them and handed them over to Abendroth. It was about five hundred dollars.

Abendroth blinked at the money in his hand and put it away. "You are far too trusting, Jesse Stockholm. What if I had plans to kill you and take your money?"

"You wouldn't do that. Besides, even if you did, you wouldn't get access to the money. I wouldn't just put it in my bag. It's secured behind an encrypted compartment of the bag. It's all courtesy of my father's technology." At Abendroth's raised eyebrow, he explained further. "He never did get around to releasing it to the public, Elias."

"You're a smart boy." The man considered him for a moment, his raised eyebrows making him look even more intense. "Maybe even smarter than your father."

The man turned away from him, and Jesse released the breath he had been holding. While Abendroth had spoken, he kept on expecting people in black to jump out from the corners and kill him. Maybe they would have just shot him in the head. Jesse had no idea where he had gotten the guts to talk like he just did, but he was glad he had.

"I'm not going to kill you. I need science more than you could imagine." Abendroth's voice jolted him from his thoughts, and he paid more attention to the man. "Most people in my field of study have no qualms with taking a life, or two. But I've never been able to stomach that idea. What makes me different from the Nazis in this same country, some hundred years ago, if I go about killing people? What people like Joseph Mengele did, all in the name of science, of discovery, all that is in no way excused."

Abendroth's face was grim, and Jesse believed him. For all that he had heard about the man's belief in time travel, he had never heard anything about Abendroth getting involved with shady business.

"Will you get help from others?" Jesse was referring to scientists like Abendroth, those who worked in the dark and got funds from people like Jesse.

"That remains to be seen." Abendroth was working on the teleportation technology attached to the time machine itself.

Jesse took a seat and rifled through his bag. "Oh, I brought breakfast for you! I forgot about it when you all but threatened me with death." Jesse could not help but glare at the back of Abendroth's head. He did not even bother changing his expression when the man turned to him.

"So, you have a sense of humor, after all." Abendroth only smiled at him and walked over to examine his plate of food. "You have good taste, Jesse. If you kept it on the table just to your left, I would appreciate it even more."

Jesse walked over to the table and dropped the food. "What do you mean by that? Of course, I have a sense of humor. It's just been difficult for me to be who I was before all this." He gestured vaguely around the room, but he was talking about what he had been through in the past year.

"And what made you do all this?" Abendroth's attention was on him, his eyes curious. "If I remember correctly, you had a fixation for an American artist. No, I am not as out of touch with the world as you must have assumed."

"Yes, Elvis Presley."

"It must have been a change for you, dressing like this." Abendroth gestured to his clothing.

"You have no idea. I didn't want anyone to recognize me. It would be so easy to stick out like a sore thumb if I dressed up as Elvis." Abendroth nodded, and Jesse wondered how the man could just understand and not mock him. "But my dad and I, we didn't agree on the way I dressed or looked. He always argued with my mom about how she raised me. She was the one who introduced me to music. The first time she played Elvis' song was when I was two. I don't remember, but she told me how excited I was. She said I danced along, doing whatever move my little brain could fathom. I must have fallen in love with his music that day."

"So, you want to go to the past to meet him?" Abendroth did not look like he minded Jesse's ramblings.

"Something like that. I do intend to meet him, but I'm also going to be him."

CHAPTER 5

The silence that followed his words lasted for about ten seconds – just long enough to allow it to become awkward – when Elias decided to speak.

"I see I was right when I said that, in your case, it might not be such a good thing to be different." Elias fixed his unwavering gaze on Jesse and shook his head. "Do you understand what–"

"I know the implications of what I want to do. What I'm *going* to do." And Jesse hated the way Elias looked at him at that moment. It was a look not too different from the one his father gave him whenever he saw him. Whenever he was reminded of who his son was. "I'm not a child. I know the consequences, and you've told me what's going to happen when I leave. I can't come back. I can't see my mom. I *know*."

His voice cracked on the last word, and Jesse hated that it did. He put his face in his hands and smoothed his hands down his face. He knew it would only leave tears on his cheek, but it was all he could do.

All the while, Elias watched him. It should have unnerved him, but it did not. "When I was addicted to gambling – I would say when I was a gambler, but science is something of a gamble – I would stake everything I had on something, all in the hopes of it yielding something great. Something grander than the thing I had given up, especially since I believed I was going to get it back. And in that belief came my addiction. It is because of that belief that I didn't see what I lost as something I was giving up. So, I would gamble every day, with everything I had. And I would lose. But I couldn't stop. I thought I was going to win at some point. I thought, oh, I haven't lost anything. What's the point in stopping? But I didn't think I could stop. Not really. I couldn't bear to lose. I didn't know it was okay.

This is the most I've spoken in a long time. Hopefully, it gets to you. You don't have to continue with something because it's all you've ever known. It's not worth doing a thing so that you can prove something to other people. You can quit when you want to."

"If you're not willing to do it, I could always find someone else who's willing to take my money. I know money will help speed up whatever research needs to be done." Jesse knew it was unnecessary to mention the amount of time it would take for him to find a scientist. They both knew it could venture into months. He did not even want to think about the process of getting information from his source before he even met the scientist.

"I will most likely regret this decision for a long time," Elias muttered to himself as he returned his attention to the time machine. "I try to choose to be human over being a man of science, but sometimes I fail. Today is one of those days." It occurred to Jesse that the man was most likely ashamed of his desperate choice. He knew he should have felt bad, but all it did was make him even more anxious to go to the past. He wanted to leave everything behind *except mom*.

"I know I should feel sorry for forcing your hand, but I'm too close to getting what I've always wanted."

After a few minutes, Elias stepped away from the time machine to grab the plate of food Jesse brought for him.

He took a seat across Jesse and slowly opened the plate. He visibly took in a whiff of the food as little steam escaped, and breathed out with a sigh. Even before digging in, it was quite apparent to Jesse that he was a man who enjoyed eating food. But it became even more apparent when he started eating. His first few bites were made with his eyes closed, and he accompanied them with slow chewing that almost made Jesse think he was watching a Judge in a cooking show.

It's kind of creepy watching a person eat, don't you think? Jesse always kept cards with him wherever he went. They were not as important as the few pictures he had, but they entertained him. He reached into his bag and took them out, careful to treat them with care. There were other things he could spend his money on.

"Have you kept in touch with your mother?" Jesse paused the shuffling of the cards to look at Elias. It had been a long time since someone asked him about her.

"Yeah, I try to call her when I can. But we don't talk for too long. I know she's determined to bring me back home, but that's not what I want." Jesse fiddled with a thread that had come loose from his cargo pants and shook his head. Thinking of his mom, especially now when he might as well have blackmailed his way into traveling back in time, was not going to do him any good. Yet he found himself talking about her. "If I could bring her along, I would. Liam doesn't deserve her. But this is my journey, and if she knew the reason for this entire thing, I'm almost sure she would lose her mind. She would blame herself for my decisions, and she's not at fault."

When he looked up, Elias' attention was fixed on him. Jesse had no idea when the man had finished eating, but the takeout plate was on the floor. "So, you admit your choices are problematic."

"To most people, yes. I understand that what I want to do isn't the most acceptable choice, but it's all I've ever known." He knew he would be seen as a lunatic by most people, but Jesse had long since closed his mind to the thoughts and opinions of others.

Elias stood, picking the takeout plate. He dropped it on the table he had picked it from and walked over to his computer.

"I should get to work now. Let me see what progress I can make."

"I can't wait for months for the possibility of a breakthrough." As they had talked, Jesse thought over everything. The thought of remaining in his present for one more week was unbearable.

"When do you plan on going, then?" Elias stopped tapping around on his laptop and faced Jesse. "It would be best to work toward it. Although, I highly doubt I will come up with a solution."

"Two days from now. I should get going. There are things I must do before I leave." Jesse swung his backpack across his shoulders and shrugged. "I'll see myself out."

Elias offered him a single nod, after which he returned his attention to his computer.

***

Jesse placed his notepad on the bed. He could not even begin to think of what to write. How could he express how sorry he was? How could he let her know how bad he felt for being the coward he was? He gripped the pen in his hand and shook his head.

He had to leave a message for her. Maybe he would call her, then send her a letter in the mail to let her know he was going to be gone for a long time. Jesse opened the notepad and started writing.

"Don't force it, Jesse. Just write whatever comes to your mind. Let your heart lead." He almost smacked his forehead in frustration when he realized he was talking to himself.

I don't know if you'll believe this or not, but I miss you. I know I'm an ass for not contacting you properly, and I know I'm the worst son for running away. A tear slid down his cheek and onto the page, but he hurriedly wiped it away with the back of his hand. *I love you for everything you've done for me, and don't ever forget that. I didn't leave because of you; all you've ever done is help me, and I love you for that. I've sent this mail to you because it'll most likely be the last time I'll get to talk with you in some way. I'm not dying. I promise. Look, I'll send a picture with this letter so that you'll know I'm not lying. I love you, mom. Tell Rosetta I'm thinking of her. I love you too, Rosetta.*

As an afterthought, he wrote: *PS it's me, Jesse.* He tossed the pen to the right and laid down, releasing a huge sigh the moment his back touched the bed. He brought his hand to his forehead and placed the back of his palm over his eyes. *It wouldn't be too bad if all this could just be done with.* And with that thought in his mind, Jesse fell asleep.

It was barely a few minutes past noon when he woke up. The scratching sound from above called for his attention, but he was practically used to it. Despite the apartment's 'strict' no pets policy, the woman who lived in the apartment above Jesse's still managed to have a dog. Jesse was almost a hundred percent sure that everyone in the apartment complex knew about the dog.

He got up from the bed and stretched his limbs. There was no time to sit around doing nothing. He had to get lunch and take a picture of himself to send to his mom. Plus, he had already made up his mind to call her after he sent the letter. Jesse gathered up his things and arranged them in his bag, making sure to pack his pen.

His first stop was two subways over; just by the corner of the subway was a man who owned a Polaroid camera. For reasons Jesse could not understand, the man at the train station made some money by taking pictures of random people. It had never appealed to Jesse, but he needed his photo taken. At the subway, he boarded the train and got down at his stop. As he expected, the man was just around the corner. He appeared to be scanning the room for something. As Jesse walked over, the man fixed his attention on him and raised his camera. He took a picture before he let the hand holding the camera fall to his side.

"Hello." The man greeted him in German and tacked a friendly smile at the end.

"Hello. I was wondering if you could take my picture," Jesse quickly rushed in to clarify what he meant when the man started raising his camera to eye level. "A proper one. Sorry, didn't mean to offend if I did. I want a picture, as I am now." He gestured to himself and let his mouth curve into a natural smile.

"But unexpected ones are the best. Everyone knows that. Here, look at this." He gestured for Jesse to move closer to him and tilted the camera upward. Jesse came closer and leaned down, letting his eyes scan the picture. It was beautiful. He looked like he had been caught doing something he had not wanted anyone to see.

"This is good." He did not know when the words slipped out of his mouth, but they were nothing short of the truth. He knew the man's rates; he could afford to buy two pictures. Besides, the rest of his money would be used to aid Elias' research. "How about you take another picture? I'll take both of the pictures."

"You'll pay for the second one. The first picture is free – I took it for the sake of art. Okay, stand over there." Jesse walked a few feet away from the man and smiled at the camera. He watched the man fiddle with a few buttons before he finally took the picture.

Jesse walked over to the man and waited as he shook the films. "I should have seen it before you developed it."

The man's eyebrows raised so high; his entire face looked comical at that moment. "I forgot about that. Do you want to take another?"

"No, it's not necessary." Jesse brought out the cash from his pocket and gave it to the man. His stomach grumbled, but he planned to eat after he was done with everything he needed to do.

"Why don't you take a seat?" Jesse looked up to see the subway photographer waving the two pictures at him. The man's camera hung safely around his neck.

"No, I'm good. The pictures have developed." The man flipped the pictures so that they faced him and nodded. "Thank you for the pictures." With that, Jesse moved on to the post office.

The post office was just a few blocks from the subway. Jesse organized the letter, fixed it alongside the two pictures of himself, and dropped it off. The mail could get to her in less than a week, but that was if there were no complications.

As he stepped out of the post office, he took a deep breath of fresh air and let it out slowly. It was time to speak with his mom. He walked at a brisk pace with his head down and made his way down the street. After a couple of turns, he entered a store and walked straight to the counter.

Jesse's way of acknowledging the presence of the man at the counter was a simple nod that the man reciprocated. He tapped his fingers on the counter as the cashier, who also doubled as a salesman, searched for what he needed. He finally stopped drumming his fingers when the cashier placed the burner phone beside his hand.

"Thanks," Jesse mumbled as he reached into the pocket of his cargo pants to pay for the burner. He grabbed the phone, nodded at the cashier, and left the store.

All that's left is lunch. A quick stop at a nearby restaurant and Jesse bought enough lunch for two people. Käsespätzle was his favorite German meal because it reminded him of mac and cheese, and the memories that came with it. Sometimes, he remembered how much mac and cheese he ate as a kid. It was at times like that that he remembered his mom even more.

✳✳✳

Jesse set down the first plate of food with a satisfied smile. He still was not sure about whether or not he should eat the second plate, or save it for dinner. Chances are, he would not be motivated to leave the apartment, or talk with anyone to order takeout, after his conversation with his mom. He quickly dialed the number he had memorized by heart and waited anxiously. She answered the call after the third ring.

"Hello?"

"Mom. Hey, it's me." After a second or two of silence, he adds, "it's Jesse."

"I know what your voice sounds like, Jesse. But is it just me, or does it sound deeper than it was the last time you called?"

"Maybe. Puberty?" Jesse let out an awkward laugh and smiled. "I hope I didn't wake you up. It's morning over there, isn't it?"

"Yeah, it's just past seven. So, what have you been up to? I would've called, but I've figured out by now that you don't want to be tracked." Jesse let out a sigh and scrubbed his hand through his hair. "Jesse, I don't know if you got yourself into trouble. No, I don't think you got yourself into trouble. Why won't you just come home?"

It was never simple for long. Most of the time, their calls would start comfortable and carefree, but, as they talked, she would talk about how he should return home.

"I'm not in trouble, mom. I don't even – what kind of trouble could I even be in? I just had to leave. I'm sorry I didn't take you along with me; I wanted you to come with me. It's just; this is my journey." He knew she would not understand what he was talking about. And that would only make her ask more questions.

"You never told me that you wanted to do anything like this. I could've supported you. The only thing you were interested in was music, and that's even too unspecific. The only thing you showed interest in was Elvis, and you can't exactly manage his shows."

That was when he decided to tell her. He could not leave her for years, wondering and not knowing where he was or what he was doing.

"No, I can't manage his shows here. But what if I could meet him?" She made a sound as if to ask a question, but he continued talking. "Mom, dad invented machines for teleportation. And for years, I followed his research closely, and I looked up scientists. Some of them work behind the government's eye, and they create things."

"Jesse, what are you talking about?" His mom sounded a bit hesitant to hear his response.

"I'm talking about time travel, mom. I met a scientist – well, actually, I searched for him – who has spent years working on a machine for time travel. Mom, he is brilliant. The crazy part is that there are people like him, but the government doesn't want to fund their research."

"Jesse." Her firm voice broke through his rambling and centered his thoughts on her once more. "Tell me you don't plan on time traveling. Tell me you haven't been sponsoring some underground scientist in the hope that he will master time travel."

"I can't tell you that. Eli - the man - already built the machine before I met him." He knew she would not appreciate his sad attempt at humor.

"You can't go back in time, Jesse."

"The machine works, mom. I just want to meet him. I want to see what he was like." *I want to be him.* He could not tell her his true intentions because she would try to stop him even more. He could not bear to hear her voice as she told him how disappointed he made her because of his decision.

"But you have a life here–"

"Not really. That could be my new life."

"You don't plan on coming back, do you?" The silence that followed her words was almost deafening.

"No. The time machine can only take me to the past. It can't bring me back." He could not even imagine how sad she felt at the moment, and it was all because of him.

"When are you leaving?" Somehow, she knew he would not be dissuaded.

"Two days from now. Mom, I'm not going to change my mind."

"Call me tomorrow, okay? I need some time to be calm. I love you. I'll tell Rosetta you called."

"I love you, mom. Tell Rosetta that I miss her." A sniffle was the only indication that she heard him before the line went silent.

CHAPTER 6

"What exactly do you plan on doing when you get there? How long have you thought of this, Jesse? I'm your mom and I didn't even know." Lisa Stockholm was frantic, and for good reason. Jesse understood her fear. He knew she would be hysteric; it did not matter that it was a day after he told her about his plan.

"Mom, it's not your fault. You had nothing to do with this." He tried his best to sound reasonable, and not patronising. His mom hated it when people patronised her.

"How can you even say that? I introduced you to his music. How could I not have known? Why didn't you tell me, Jesse?"

"I knew you were only going to try to get me to stay. And that's what you're doing now. You didn't do anything wrong." They were silent for a few seconds, both deep in thought. "I've wanted to do this for so long, mom. I've thought about it since sophomore year."

"I don't want to guilt trip you but, I'm here. I'm your mom and I'm here for you." He knew what she was asking, what she was saying: *Isn't she enough? Isn't their reality good enough?*

But it wasn't. Not really. Not for him.

"I know you're here for me, but I have to live my life. I want to live my life." He paused, giving her the opportunity to speak if she wanted to. "I'm going to do this, mom. And I know you won't like it. I know you don't want it, and you might even hate me for my terrible decision–"

"I could never hate you." His mom's voice was as tender as could be, when she interrupted him. She sounded like she had been crying quietly as he talked, and he hated to think that he must be the reason she even knew how to do that. He hated that he knew he was the reason she could do that. *All these months I've been away from home; she must have cried herself to sleep.*

"If you don't hate me, then…" Jesse let his voice trail off before tacking on, "I don't understand. How could you not hate me for this?"

"You're my son, Jesse. I couldn't hate you if I wanted to. I know there are mothers out there who hate their children, and even went as far as killing them, but I've never understood how they do that. You are so lovable. And you're amazing. Plus, you have good taste in music." She let out a laugh and followed it up with a sniffle. Jesse smiled and cleaned the tears which had trailed down to his cheeks.

The noise started immediately after. He wanted to continue the conversation, but it persisted. "Mom, I think something's going on. Hold on for a second, let me find out what's going on."

"Okay. Be careful, it's getting really noisy."

A loud knock on the door startled him. He stayed quiet, just in case the person wanted to kill him for whatever reason. But the person knocked again, and it was louder this time. "There's a fire in the building, and we all have to leave."

He hesitated, unsure whether or not it was smart of him to open the door. Voices from outside the room clashed as they repeated variations of the same message: *There's a fire! Apartment 2 is on fire. Get up, and get out of your rooms.* Jesse quickly grabbed his bag and unlocked his door. The woman who had knocked on his door had left but, he could not help but wonder what made her choose to help him. He was almost sure he had never spoken to her.

His burner phone was in his hand as he jogged out of the apartment. There were people littered outside the apartment. Many held bags in their hands, and it struck Jesse then that they were not so different from one other. Most of them had their entire lives contained in a backpack, as did he. *If mom could see me right now, she would lose it.*

"Mom." Jesse remembered that she was still on the other end of the line, and quickly put the phone to his ear.

"Jesse."

"Mom."

"What's going on? What happened? Are you safe?"

"Yes, it was just a fire. One of the apartments, which is far from mine," he added the last part for her benefit.

"When will they let you back in?" From the look of things, he was not sure they would be let back in any time soon. The state of the building would be seen as uninhabitable, as long as it remained this way. And it would be more of a loss on the part of the landlord to let them stay in the building, giving the fact that the government could shut it down for months if they found out.

"I don't know. I don't think they will. At least not today." Or tomorrow. A government official would have to check the building, and objectively decide if it would be hazardous for people to keep living in it. "I have somewhere to stay. You don't have to be worried. I can stay with the scientist."

He did not have to elaborate. She knew who he meant when he referred to a scientist.

"Is it safe?"

"Yes, it's safe. He's a good man."

✳✳✳

Elias ushered Jesse in, and locked the door behind him. It was afternoon and the hallways leading to Elias's research lab were illuminated so, Jesse could walk without having to be extra careful.

"I wasn't expecting you today. It's a pleasant surprise, I hope." Elias looked back at him, before he continued walking.

"Yes, I know. Well, the apartment I'm staying at is considered a hazard now. There was a fire in one of the rooms." Jesse assumed Elias would fill in the blanks and break the silence, but he remained silent. "And I don't have anywhere else to go. This is the only place I could think of. I would've gone to a motel or something but I don't have that kind of money. Not anymore."

"If you want to rest or sleep now, the sleeping area isn't too far from here. There's a single bed, but I can assemble another." Jesse was stunned into silence. It had been a long time since someone had looked out for him. And all of a sudden, in a day, two people he barely knew had looked out for him.

Elias must have taken his silence for displeasure because he said, "if you don't want to sleep in there, you can sleep wherever you want."

"No, it's not that. Thank you for the bed. You don't have to assemble the bed; I can just sleep on the foam."

"It's an inflatable bed." Jesse noticed how Elias' posture became relaxed the moment he walked into his lab.

This is what I want for myself. This is what I'm going to get in the past.

"I just need to call my mom."

Elias gave him directions to the sleeping area, and he prepared his heart for the inevitable goodbye.

***

Jesse's tight grip on the messenger bag he bought earlier in the day with the little money he had left was a clear indication of the importance of its contents. He would have gone with his backpack, but he knew he would stick out like a sore thumb. Modern backpacks, especially the ones with little modifications such as Jesse's, had not been invented in the 1950s.

"It would be better if you got there in the morning or mid-afternoon. That way, people are more likely to see you and you can hitch a ride." Elias hurried around the lab, flicking a few buttons here and there. Jesse wondered what exactly he was doing because the man hardly ever slept, and he must have gone through the process earlier.

Maybe it's nerves. That would explain it, but Jesse did not think Elias was as nerve wracked as he was. He was going back in time, and he would never return to the present he had known all his life. What were the odds that Elias would discover a way to fix the limitations of the time machine during his lifetime? Elias was not the oldest scientist Jesse had ever met, neither was he a strapping young lad. Jesse believed he was in his 50s, going on 60s. That meant that he would soon lose even more energy, despite having the passion to continue with science.

"I will show you that the machine works. I should've done that earlier but, amidst all the excitement, it crossed my mind. And you didn't ask. Again, you are far too trusting, Jesse Stockholm." Elias paused to look at him, then wiped his brow with a face towel. "The world will chew you up and spit you out if you continue this way."

Jesse continued watching him but, internally, he was face palming. *How could I have forgotten to see a demonstration? Elias could have scammed me, and I would have been unable to do anything because I would have been floating endlessly in time.* Elias gestured for him to come closer and he did. He was holding up a piece of paper, and a pen was in his left hand. Elias wrote something down on the paper and gave it to Jesse.

It read: *Jesse is doing this. You are Jesse.*

"What's this for?" Jesse asked, handing Elias the piece of paper.

"This is the proof that all this," he gestured to his lab, "works. I have enough power to make it stable, so it's fine. That was one of the things I spent your money on."

Jesse watched the time machine, and he wondered how the portal would look like. Elias held the paper in his hand and flicked a couple of switches by the side of the portal. But nothing happened. It still looked like a regular, oval-shaped door. Until Elias threw the paper into the space within the time machine.

Jesse had expected the paper to appear on the other end, but it did not. There was a crackle, and a lightning-like silver matter that expanded within the time machine before reducing into nothing. Then there was nothing. The paper was gone. Jesse was so stunned, he stumbled backward. It seemed like the paper was fried, but the usual smell that lingered in a place after something had been burned was absent.

He was about to question Elias when the time machine came to life. It looked like a picture of a field of tall grass – except it was not a picture. There, not too far from him, but not too close that he could reach, was the paper fluttering in the wind. It landed on the grass and swayed slowly. But his attention was quickly snagged away when he heard the low rumble of a car. He could see the car approaching.

All of a sudden, everything disappeared, leaving the time machine looking as normal as possible.

"It wouldn't be wise to let the driver of the car, or its inhabitants, see the portal. There would be too many complications if that happened." Elias' explanation made every bit of sense, and Jesse understood.

"Okay."

"Here, take these for nausea. There may be other side effects, but none will be long-lasting. You don't have to worry about any of that." Jesse took the bottle from Elias, along with the bottle of water he offered. "Take two of this."

Jesse put some water in his mouth and quickly swallowed the drugs. He had always hated the taste of drugs in his mouth, even the sweet tasting ones. Elias handed him another bottle and told him to take a single pill, and he did that quickly.

"It's time, then?" He tugged on the messenger bag in a bid to ease his nerves, but it was pointless.

Elias only nodded in response to his question because he was occupied with starting up the time machine. However, he paused before he flicked the last button. "You are a good person, in your way. You love your mother, and you care for people. This is a decision and it will have consequences. Those consequences will be negative and positive, and they will change the lives of people. Good luck, Jesse Stockholm." And with that, he flicked the last button.

Jesse walked the remaining distance to the time machine. His hands were shaking, but that could have been one of the side effects of the drugs.

"Thank you, Elias. You've helped me so much." He looked at the man, barely resisting the urge to hug him. He had been without proper human contact for so long. But he needed to leave. Elias offered him a nod which he reciprocated, then he stepped into the time machine.

It felt like he was being thrown across time, and rather roughly at that. He could not open his eyes because it felt like they would be ripped out of his eye sockets if he did. So, he opened his mouth and let out his scream of terror as he was taken from his present to the past. There was always the possibility of giving up the content of his stomach, and that scared him. *I'm going to throw up. I'm going to throw–*

Jesse stumbled as his right leg sunk into the blades of tall grass, and he quickly put his hands out in front of him but all he could grab was grass. Jesse groaned as he pushed himself off the ground. He quickly dusted his clothes which were a milder, and more acceptable, variation of the kind he was used to wearing.

"At least I know the road isn't too far from here, but that's if I start walking now." The sun was high in the sky, suggesting it was afternoon. Jesse trudged through the field of grass and, with every step he took, he prayed the road was just a step away.

He had been walking for a minute or so when something fluttered in the wind to his left. It looked like the paper Elias had tossed through the portal earlier. Had it just been a few minutes since he had seen the man? It felt like hours had passed since then, what with him being taken through time.

Jesse grabbed the paper and carefully put it in his bag. It would be part of the mementos that he had from his former present. *This is my new present. I am now Jesse Stockholm, a teenager in the early 1950s.*

Finally, Jesse pushed through the grass and onto the side of the road. He had no idea where he was, or where he was headed, but he kept on walking. A few minutes later, he heard the tell-tale rumble of a car engine driving up the road. He turned and watched the car. It was the only car he had seen since he landed, and he would have to hitchhike. Jesse raised his hand to flag down the car and, surprisingly, the driver idled the car onto the side of the road. Jesse quickly walked over and leaned down to see the driver.

The driver looked to be in his late twenties, but Jesse was not so sure. "Good day, sir. Would you mind giving me a ride into town?"

The man examined him quickly but, he must have been pleased with Jesse's demeanour because he said, "get in, then."

"Thank you." Jesse quickly got in, and closed the door. He put the seatbelt in place and leaned against the seat.

"So where are you coming from? There's miles and miles of nothing but the road, so you must have been walking for some time." The man flexed his fingers on the steering wheel.

"I haven't been walking for too long, actually." Jesse deflected the man's question and silently hoped it would not be noticed. "Where exactly is this? I lost my map some hours ago."

"Didn't you see any sign on your way?" The man let out a chuckle when Jesse shook his head. "You must have come from the sky, then."

You have no idea.

"I wasn't really paying attention."

"Well, we're in Memphis, Tennessee." Memphis was the location of Sun Records; the record label that signed Elvis Presley.

"I've never been to Memphis, but I'm going to Sun Records studio. I don't know if you know where that is. Maybe you can drop me off on the way to wherever you're going."

"Today must be your lucky day. I'm headed to Sun Records as well." The man, and Jesse was getting tired of thinking of him as a person without a name, shook his head at Jesse and smiled.

And truly, Jesse could not believe his luck.

CHAPTER 7

"You work at Sun Records? That must be interesting." Jesse wanted to know who he was, but it was not reasonable to just jump right into that question. The man seemed like someone with his fair share of desperate people who wanted to sing. "All I've ever known is science, for the most part."

The man was quiet as if he wanted to know whether Jesse was baiting him. But he spoke after about thirty seconds. "Science, huh? That must be fascinating."

You have no idea. I'm literally from the future.

"I suppose it can be fascinating. My father was a scientist, but his father before him was not. Somehow, my father got it into his head that I must venture into science." Jesse was surprised at how quickly and easily he spun his web of lies. Maybe it was easy to do because it was not so different from his situation with his father.

"Fathers are usually a challenge for everyone. What's your name, then?" The man casually slipped out the question, and Jesse cursed himself for not thinking everything through. He was not sure if he should use his real name, or make something up.

"My name's Jesse Stockholm."

"Stockholm? Are you Swiss or something?" Jesse shook his head in disagreement with the question. "Well, I'm Sam Philips, Jesse. It's been a pleasure meeting you."

But Jesse's attention was no longer on the man's words. Sam Philips. Sam Philips. The man was the founder of Sun Records. He was lucky enough to be in the same car as the man, and he had to make this work.

"Sam Philips. You're the founder of Sun Records., You should listen to my music, sir." Jesse projected every confidence he could muster into his voice. If he could get Sam to listen, he would score big. All of Elvis' songs were works of art, and he knew he sounded amazing while singing them.

"You're a musician? I thought you were a scientist." Sam sounded like he was losing interest in him and fast.

"I was a scientist, but I quit to focus on music. That's why my father and I have this huge rift between us. I don't have my guitar here, or anywhere near her, but I can show you." Jesse was starting to sound desperate. He knew it, but there was only so much he could do to stop his desperation from being too obvious.

"Why should I give you a chance? Do you know how many people want to get signed by Sun Records?"

"I'm better than the rest of them. I will start singing right now if that is what takes to show you." Jesse was only half-joking. He was ready to do almost anything, as long as it got Sam Philips listening to his rendition of Elvis' songs.

Jesse opened his mouth, ready to start singing, but Sam stopped him. "If you're as good as you say you are, meet some producers with me. We're getting closer to the studio." And sure enough, Jesse could see the building with the Sun Records written boldly across the top.

They were both quiet as Sam idled into a free parking space. Jesse could only imagine how different their thoughts were. He believed Sam's thoughts were similar to this: *how do I get this kid to leave me alone? I suppose I should just let him show us what he's made of.*

"We're here." Sam stepped out of the car, and Jesse did too, closing the door behind him. Jesse shouldered his bag and maintained the tight grip he had on it as he followed Sam into the building.

It was obvious to Jesse that Sam had a destination in mind because he barely stopped to interact with people. Jesse quickly guessed Sam was taking him to the producers. Soon, they entered a room that looked more like a lounge. There were three men already in the room and, although they must have been discussing before Sam walked in, they all greeted him cheerfully.

It did not take long for the producers to notice Jesse. "Who's the young man? You look like you just ended a marathon, kid."

"I feel like I just ran a marathon," Jesse remarked, and the men chuckled.

"I found him by the roadside," Sam turned to Jesse and smiled as if to tell him not to take offense. "Seems like he landed from the sky. He says he can sing, so I brought him here to sing for us."

"They can all sing." One of the men seemed less than enthusiastic about the whole thing, but Jesse could not blame him.

"Let's hear him out. I have a feeling about this one." Sam was quick to come to his rescue, and Jesse appreciated him for that.

"I don't know if there's a spare acoustic guitar I can play as I sing." Sam walked to a door that Jesse assumed led to an inner room and, when he returned, he held an acoustic guitar in his hand. Sam handed the guitar to Jesse and sat in the corner of the room.

Jesse positioned the guitar correctly and started strumming, getting a feel of things. He started strumming a more upbeat tempo to Arthur Crudup's *That's All Right*, just as Elvis had done when he recorded the song. The producers were getting lost in the music, and he had not started singing.

Jesse felt his mouth curve into a smile as he belted out the lyrics to the song.

***

The producers were outright dancing when Jesse stopped singing. He knew they were beyond impressed. Their enthusiastic clapping, alongside their nodding and insistent conversation on how refreshing his rendition of the song was, all these let him know just how much he had impressed them.

"You have talent, boy." They smiled at him, but all he did was nod. They were not going to sign him to the record; Sam Philips was.

"You've got an eye, Sam. I don't know how you do it, but you've got an eye for this kind of thing."

"You mean he's got an ear for it."

"This is the first time I've heard him sing. I had no idea he was this good, gentlemen." Sam rubbed his hands against his pants and stood up. He walked over to Jesse and reached out for a handshake. Jesse obliged him readily. "You've got some talent, Jesse. It's not every day the producers and I hear unique voices. Now, your kind of voice will definitely pull a crowd."

"More than a crowd. The entire country is going to be rooting for you if we play this right."

"Gentlemen," Sam addressed the producers who were still talking among themselves, "we don't want to scare him off with this kind of talk."

One of the producers – Jesse thought he recognized him from pictures he had seen online – scoffed at Sam's words. "We're not going to chase him away, Sam."

"Look, how about you go home or lodge at a motel, and you return tomorrow?" Sam returned his attention to Jesse once more. "You need rest, and we have a lot to discuss as regards your music career."

"I would do that, but I don't have money. I came here, empty-handed. I just knew I had to get to Sun Records and bedazzle you with my voice. I don't know if you can let me sleep here tonight. I can sort myself out tomorrow."

"Oh, you can't sleep in the studio. Normally, I wouldn't do this, but I can see how tired you are. You can stay at my house, at least until you find somewhere you can call yours." Jesse was shocked at the offer, and his shock must have shown on his face because Sam quickly assured him. "It's just something I would want people to do if I ever find myself in a situation similar to yours. Right now, I'm treating you like my younger brother."

"Thank you for this. I promise you won't regret this decision."

"Oh, I know, kid."

"To show my gratitude, I'll repay you for this generosity with the money I make as an artiste under your record label." Sam laughed at Jesse's words and shook his head.

"I admire your confidence, Jesse Stockholm."

✳✳✳

Jesse took a sip from the bottle of water and put it down. He had been in the studio for three hours now, and he had to be careful to avoid straining his voice. Sam was talking with John, one of the producers Jesse met on his first day in Sun Records. John was his favorite person, after Sam, in Sun Records. He was in his thirties, but he reminded Jesse of a teenage boy going through puberty.

"Jesse, get over here." John gestured him over with his gangly arm. He ran his hand through his hair and sighed. Jesse had never seen John's hair neatly combed. He knew John probably brushed it at home, but by the time he got to the studio, his hair would be disheveled because he always ran his hand through it.

John patted his shoulder when he got to them. "You're doing great, Jesse. Your voice blends well with the musical instruments."

"Thank you, John. That means a lot coming from you."

"It's pretty obvious that you love performing, and that'll make the fans love you. We're not going to record every song you have right away." John nodded at Sam to take over the conversation.

"You're a new act, and people don't know who you are. It won't be a smart move to introduce you with an album, so we plan to release *That's All Right*. When folks listen to it, they'll love it."

"Okay. I'm okay with that. I trust the process." Their choice of action was in line with the contract Jesse had signed the day after he arrived in Memphis, so there was no reason for him to be worried. He knew little to nothing about Tennessee law in 1954, but he told himself that he would read up on it.

It occurred to him at that moment that he could no longer access the internet for whatever information he needed. He would have to go to a library.

"You can hang around or take a cab to my house. There's nothing else for you to do today. Have a good rest."

"I think I'll hang around." Jesse's thoughts quickly strayed to his mother. She had a set routine for Saturdays, and she always tried to involve him in it. Weekends were spent differently here. He was not sure of the activities people engage in on the weekend, but he knew yoga was out of the question.

Sundays were for going to church; of that, he was certain. A lightbulb went off in his head. Elvis was in Tennessee, and he attended church on Sundays with his family.

"Is there a church called Assembly of God anywhere near here?" Jesse called out to the room, hoping someone would answer.

"Yes, there's one not too far from my house. It's walking distance, even." It was Sam who answered him. "I didn't take you for a religious man."

"I'm not. There's someone I want to see," Jesse shrugged, hoping he seemed calm.

"Is it a girl? You work fast, Jesse." There was collective laughter as people in the studio heard Sam's words.

Jesse mimicked the sound of their laughs and shook his head to show them that he took it all in good stride. "It's not a girl. Just an old friend."

✳✳✳

Jesse had never felt so out of place. In all his nineteen years, he had gone to church twice. His family had never been religious. Rosetta was the reason he had ever entered a church. She invited him and his mom regularly, but they never went.

Most of the church's congregation was looking at him like he was something out of a movie, but he was used to that. Jesse had taken to dressing as he used to, with the only exception being his lack of sideburns. The sideburns would take some time to grow, but he knew to be patient.

"Uncle Elvis?" Someone tugged on his shirtsleeve, and he turned to see a girl.

"I'm sorry. I thought you were Uncle Elvis." The girl's mother hurried over to take her away with an apologetic smile.

"I'm sorry about this."

"It's no problem," but the woman was already hurrying to take a seat at the other end of the church.

At least I know Elvis is a member of this church.

Jesse zoned out for most of the service. It was the claps and tangible excitement of the congregation that brought him back to Earth. Elvis made his way to the podium with his guitar in hand.

Jesse was star struck. It had always been his dream to watch Elvis perform live; it did not matter what song he performed. Jesse was not listening to the words of the song. He was more invested in the rhythm and effortlessness of the entire performance.

The service rounded up after that, and Jesse found himself in a battle with his nerves. He could not imagine walking up to Elvis to strike a conversation. *What will I say? How do I even start? Do I just tell him how amazing he was, or do I tell him how I traveled from the future to see him?*

Jesse did his best to calm his nerves then he went to meet Elvis before he lost his calm.

"You're an amazing singer." Elvis turned to look at him. *Calm down, Jesse. Just get through this, and don't ramble.* "This is my first time in this church, and I'm probably going to come here next Sunday to hear the angels sing through you."

To hear the angels sing through you? What is he? A vessel? Jesse cringed at his words.

"Uh, thank you. We really could pass as twins if our faces were covered up." Jesse must have looked confused because Elvis rushed to explain what he meant. "My neighbor told me she saw someone who dressed like me. She said you might as well be my reflection."

"I don't know about being your reflection, but, if I sounded like you when I sing, I would never stop singing." Elvis laughed at his words, and Jesse smiled.

"It's good to get such a positive review from a new face. I've been trying to get into music. I want to do more than singing in church – not that there's anything wrong with it – but it's tough finding a label that wants more than cheating you of your money."

"I understand. I sing a little, here and there, so I know what it's like."

"Elvis Presley!" The name reverberated in the medium-sized church.

"My momma's calling. Soon she'll chase me out of the church with a stick, but that's if I don't get to her in a minute or two." Elvis slung his messenger bag across his shoulder and saluted Jesse. "I'll see you next week if you decide to come." Elvis made to leave but Jesse rammed into him in a tight embrace, nearly knocking the air out of him.

A few seconds passed before Elvis spoke. "If someone saw you, they'd think you're meeting your brother who just got back from the army for the first in years." Jesse took a moment to savour the moment, still in doubt that was really happening.

"You okay?" Elvis asked when Jesse continued to embrace him. He chuckled slightly.

"Elvis Aaron Presley!" Jesse snapped back to the present. A million thoughts had spiralled through his mind. He really went through with his plans and he'd finally met his all-time favourite star. He'd hoped somehow, he would wake from whatever dream he'd thought he was having yet he wanted assurance that it was really happening and he wasn't dreaming. That's why he'd hugged Elvis. The mention of his idol's full name had snapped him back to reality.

Elvis managed a smile. "Are you sure you're good?" Jesse nodded. *My momma's really gonna have my neck now.*

"Right." Jesse moved to the left, leaving Elvis with room to walk past him.

"Wait, what's your name?"

"Jesse." *Elvis Presley is asking for my name.* Jesse was aware that he sounded like a fangirl having a meltdown after meeting her idol, but that was because he was a fanboy meeting his idol.

"I'll see you another time, Jesse." Elvis offered him a wave and a smile; then, he was gone.

"I'll see you around." *How weird is it that I've watched nearly all of the videos online that have to do with you? Be it recording sessions in a studio, rehearsals for a performance, and the actual performances themselves.*

Jesse could imagine how the conversation would be if he told Elvis everything he knew about him.

I know you're singing in church now, but you're going to be signed to a record label in a year. Just hang in there.

What do you mean?

I mean, you're going to have millions of fans who will love you for you. Some will love you for your voice. Some will love you for your charisma, and they'll see you as someone to be like.

And what happens after that?

You become one of the kings of rock and roll. The crowds will learn every word of all your songs.

Will I be happy? Will I die happy?

I don't know if you will ever be truly happy, as I never knew you personally, but I don't think you will. I'm sorry. As for the question of whether or not you will die a happy man, you will be a legend. Some say that is enough. But it's not enough, is it?

"Maybe you won't die if I live the life you were supposed to live. Maybe you'll find fulfillment elsewhere. Maybe I'm doing you a favor by forcing you to live a simple life."

Jesse knew he was only repeating the words to himself because he did not want to be eaten up by guilt. But it was pointless.

He tried however, to look at the upside. *The whole life he had ahead of him* Abendroth had spoken of must be this life. People did say everyone had a purpose in life. This was his purpose and he was going to make the best of it.

The one good thing his father's behavior birthed was *this*. Everything all came down to this very moment and he had never been grateful his father had been such as ass.

CHAPTER 8

Jesse had spent the next few minutes walking around the church. It was his way of passing time. He wasn't ready to leave just yet. If he wanted, he could go back to the house Sam had been so kind to let him share with him. Jesse wondered if the other producers he met on the first day of his arrival to the new timeline he was present in were like Sam Phillips—kind enough to let him stay till he found his own space.

But then again, the man probably made an exception of him only because he wanted to keep him close; as much as he knew Jesse was breakthrough, he needed to bring success and fame bring success to Sun Records and himself as a producer.

Unlike the church, Rosetta had invited him and his mom to, this one lacked the bright colors and statues of Mary and the Saints, along with one of a baby Jesus and his mother Mary as Rosetta had oh-so given a full explanation the two times he attended church in his life. He'd asked the kind of service they conducted, and she'd told him they referred to it as Mass. That with a bunch of other things she went on about.

It was as though she knew that was the last time they would attend church together and not for the un-obvious reason of him leaving home, but because he found the whole religious thing a hassle. And worse, following a program for it with other people while someone recited words from a book.

"The church wasn't very big. It looked decent on the outside and just as decent on the inside. There weren't a lot of people around he noticed, but he saw the stark similarity in the behavior the people here shared with the people at Rosetta's church back home. They felt the need to greet one another and exchange pleasantries amongst themselves.

I reckon I haven't seen your face around here before. Are you a new member of our congregation?" An elderly-looking woman cornered him as he was about to make a turn to what looked to him like an entrance leading to a staircase. "But oh my, little Judy wasn't kidding when she said she saw a young man who looks and dresses just like our Elvis."

Our Elvis? They also did that here? Refer to one another as their own. They did the same at Rosetta's. He wondered if it was the same everywhere else. It meant most if not all knew what was going on in each others' lives if it was a collective behavior. Not that it mattered to him. He wasn't even religious. But he couldn't help but wonder what I'd be like.

However, that also meant they were all up in each others' business. Jesse frowned. It didn't seem like something he'd ever find himself accustomed to. Privacy was something Jesse Stockholm valued.

"Good day, ma'am." He managed a small smile. She said nothing and just looked at him. "Well, are you?" Was he what? "Are you new to the church?"? I don't believe Elvis ever mentioned a new relative coming to church". He shook his head. "We're not related."

"But that also meant they were all up in each others' business. Jesse frowned. Didn't seem like something he'd ever find himself accustomed to. Privacy was something Jesse Stockholm valued.

If I didn't know better, I'd say you are, but I'd be damned. I see his sense isn't of dressing isn't just restricted to him". She waved her frail- looking hands in the air as if looking for the right words to describe his choice of wardrobe.

She took his hand and pulled him along with her, leading him to a group of people at the far end of the church. They were laughing at something a young blonde boy said. He looked seven or thereabouts.

They all stopped laughing when they saw him. Confusion etched on all their faces. The older woman nodded and then sighed, "I had the same expression when I spotted him. The resemblance is uncanny".

"What's your name, boy?" One of the men from the crowd asked him. He had more strands of silver hairs than black, evidence the man had lived a time longer than he. The man looked to be the oldest out of everyone who gathered in front of him. The woman from earlier left his side to join the gathered crowd.

"Jesse. Jesse Stockholm".

"You from Stockholm?" Jesse wasn't sure whom, but someone from the crowd inquired. Even more so, he wasn't sure if that was an intended joke, so he shook his head and smiled instead. "Well, are you new then? To the congregation, I mean". They didn't press further about where he was from, which he was grateful for. He didn't know what he'd have said had they inquired about that. Heck, he wasn't even sure what his hometown was like at this time.

"I asked him the same question, but he said nothing." The older woman from earlier spoke up. He scratched the back of his head. Their stares were slowly getting him agitated. What if they asked him who it was? Or what his relationship with Elvis Presley was? If there was one thing Jesse Stockholm was terrible at, it was lying. He hoped with everything he had, and they'd drop the questions. He needed to leave. He wasn't sure to handle any more questions.

"No, no, I'm not. I only came by to see someone."

You look like uncle Elvis." The young blonde boy beamed at him. He was gesturing with his hands to his face the similarities in hair and sideburns. Yeah, I came here to steal his life.

If he was going to live up to the half—no, just the man Elvis Presley was, he might as well get to it. He needed to head out, to leave the company of these people who stared intently at him.

They seemed to sense his discomfort because the older man took it upon himself to disperse the crowd. Some murmured goodbyes while the rest said nothing and just went their ways.

Jesse politely called the older man aside. He needed help locating clubs that played the kind of music his idol fancied.

He should have asked Sam or one of the producers at the studio before leaving, but he'd been too excited to meet Elvis that he forgot to. He hoped the older man had the answer he was looking for.

***

He was in luck. Jesse had wasted no time in leaving the vicinity before anyone else could bombard him with questions he'd instead not answer. At least not yet. Not until he had come up with some believable tales to tell.

The old man didn't disappoint. Jesse had bothered about how he would have had to ask around had the old man been unable to give him a positive response. But he came through, and Jesse had been nothing but happy with the results.

He told him the fastest route to follow from the church. He could either take a cab or follow a shortcut. Lucky for him, there was a club not too far from the House of God he just exited. The man had even told him of some pretty good diners tourists from afar liked to visit.

A tourist. Jesse scoffed, but he was satisfied nonetheless. The man believed him when he told him he was there to tour the city. Understanding dawned on the older man when he commented on his outlook. He concluded that Elvis dressed the way the same way because he picked it up somewhere, and he believed Jesse picked it up too. It was a good sign. Maybe I'm not such a bad liar, but how long until I start to believe my lies? How long till I start living them? That's if he wasn't already.

Slowly, he grew accustomed to his new life and the new time. There were times he found it difficult adjusting. Like when he first arrived. The currencies he brought him with were very different from what they used in this time and the dates; he still hadn't gotten used to being in the 1950s. It felt weird to him and the music— not that he had a problem with it, but sometimes some songs that came on were cringe-worthy.

He followed the path the old man from the church asked him to. Now and then, he would stop by the windows of shops and diners. They seemed to fascinate him. He kept touring till he got to what looked like a bar. Jesse stood for a moment, taking the environment in before walking to the bar.

Everything here looked so different compared to his former home: the people, their demeanor, the technology, telephones, clothes—not that his dressing style hadn't been different from the get-go, music. In many ways, the music didn't bother him. After all, he was an Elvis Presley fanatic. People seemed more welcoming than those from his past.

Jesse found his situation particularly funny. In a timeline in the past, he was here, yet somehow those from the future had become his past and those from the past, his new future. He couldn't help but laugh out loud.

A young man was sitting next to him; he looked to be in his early twenties. He said nothing at first as he watched Jesse intently as he continued to laugh. "Care to share to share your cause for excitement?" By this time, Jesse has stopped laughing. The man raised his glass to Jesse. "I'm Peter."

"Jesse."

He only grinned in response, then turned to the barman and asked him to pour a shot of liquor for Jesse. I shouldn't be drinking, but he doesn't know that, and he doesn't have to. Jesse wondered if he could stomach it. If his mother could see him right now— he stopped himself. No. He was out to connect with his idol. He didn't want to waste his time dwelling on reasons he should have never left.

The two men got talking, bonding over shots of alcohol. Jesse found out Peter was twenty-two, and he managed a bar downtown. It was as though a force seemed to be on his side because the moment Jesse fed him the lie of being a tourist hunting for clubs that played rhythm and blues, black and white gospel songs, Peter wasted no time in suggesting his bar. Thankfully, Peter owned a car.

"Why don't you drink at your bar?"

"I do, but I'd rather just drink somewhere else, you know." Peter led the way as the two men went outside. Well, I'd be damned. "Is that a Muntz?" Jesse knew his face was one of both astonishment and disbelief. But it wasn't because he was doing pretty well for his age.

Back home, it wasn't something rare. In the future time, he'd seen various brands of cars, but he'd never seen a Muntz before.

This young man was doing pretty well for a twenty-two-year-old. At his age, he already owned a bar and drove his car. in this time, he knew it wasn't something that quickly accomplished.

His new friend wasn't sure if he was joking or not. "You're serious? You've never seen this before?" Jesse shook his head frantically. I've only seen these on TVs, magazines, and the net, never in person.

"The net? You mean like an actual net?" Right. He did it again. Using slang, most people would most likely not understand. Jesse waved him off. "I meant I'd not seen one this close." His companion didn't press further. He ushered Jesse to get in, and they drove off.

***

Jesse heard the jazz music blasting from the club before they'd even stepped out of the car.

"I hope you know how to party," Peter grinned. He patted Jesse on the back as they stepped into the club. Jesse followed as his new acquaintance led them to an empty table. Both men ordered the same thing from before.

Moments passed before Jesse started to feel the effect of the alcohol. He wasn't drunk, but he felt tipsy enough to want to hit the dance floor. If this was how Elvis felt whenever he felt inspired as he made music, Jesse wanted to feel more of what he is, so he danced. His steps weren't in sync with the music, but it was so terrible. I almost lost my mind by Ivory Joe Hunter came on. His unconventional dancing skills caught the attention of most in the room, but that didn't stop him. There were cheers, laughter, and whistling from various ends of the room.

All the attention in the room was on him now. He felt a stripper giving a special dance for the audience to watch. For one, he knew the reason why he was still dancing was solely due to the beautiful blonde girl that caught his eyes now had hers fixed intently on him. She looked amused. He'd noticed her in between his drink with Peter, and he'd watched her since then. Now she pleased watching him dance.

He gestured for her to join him. They danced together for what seemed like a long time. "Where'd you learn to dance like that?" she looked eager to hear his response. "I'm not quite sure myself." Peter seemed to have disappeared, but Jesse dismissed the thought.

Jesse had inquired about her name in the middle of their dance. Dorothy, she'd told him. He led them back to the seat he'd exited from.

Whenever she asked him anything personal, he would evade the question by throwing it back at her. It wasn't until she asked about his favorite type of music and artist that he responded.

"Well, I know someone who sings pretty well. He's not mainstream. Not yet, at least, but he's my favorite artist. I like rhythm and blues, jazz sometimes and gospel. You know, I'm a pretty decent artist myself." He'd only just met Dorothy, but he found himself wanting to impress her. Jesse told Dorothy of his recent signing to Sun Records. Of course, that piqued her interest. She was passionate about music, just like he was.

The record label had only just started. So, they weren't that big of a deal just yet. He would be the one to change that, though. He would make sure of it.

Jesse scanned the crowd Peter, and almost immediately, he saw him. He quickly excused himself from the table and went to Peter. "I won't belong. I'm going out for a walk." It must have been his habit because Peter said nothing but raised a glass to him like he did when they met earlier.

Jesse walked back to his table. Together, he and the beautiful blonde exited the bar.

He said nothing in the first ten seconds they stepped out. If they were taking a walk, his thoughts would need to be recollected first.

Dorothy must have mistaken his silence for something else when she said, "is something the matter?" She paused and looked up at him.

Dorothy creased her eyebrows, a worried expression taking over her face. Mom. His mother did that whenever she got sick with worry . Furrowing her eyebrows while she touched her palm to her face. "I-, I'm fine." He choked out. He didn't mean to.

The blonde girl didn't buy the lie. She shook her head. "Tell me, please. I want to help you." *There you again— reminding me of the one person I hate that I left behind.* She touched his arm lightly when he ignored her. "Jesse?"

He was in for it. Jesse didn't need a soul to spell it out for him. What? He'd only met this girl for like an hour plus, but he was already falling deep. It was the first time she'd said his name out loud. Even when he'd introduced himself, she didn't repeat it. Hearing her say it now turned him to mush.

He told himself it was because no one paid him attention in his past. But even he knew that was a lie. Before he'd been ousted as a weirdo for his obsession with Elvis Presley, he'd had friends. Females and males alike. He'd also crushes and even had his feelings reciprocated, but neither had felt like this.

The beautiful woman who stood in front of him was different from the women he'd met. And if he was being honest, he'd barely known many except his mom and Rosetta and maybe that was why he felt this way or maybe it was the fact that she was as passionate about music as he was or that she reminded him greatly of his mother.

Whatever the reason, he wanted to explore more with her by his side.

"It's nothing. You just remind me so much of someone." He took her dainty hands in his. "Someone who means the world to me, though she's not here with me, you managed to remind me of her. Her face softened. From the hour he met down to that very moment, Jesse had never seen her look more innocent. Barely two hours together and he'd already fallen for the beautiful blonde woman in front of him.

CHAPTER 9

Jesse was living the life he wanted. The life of Elvis Presley, and he wished one person was here to see him the most- Liam Stockholm.

The words his father said on his tenth birthday that he could never forget; *you'll never be Elvis Presley*. Yet, here he was, proving his father wrong and doing one of the things he'd probably said with the most convictions in himself. Yet, Jesse had won the hearts of most of the audience. He was living the life he never thought he'd live. The life of his idol, his number one star. He was living in fame. His young life was blissful.

He had a girlfriend whom he loved dearly and who loved him back. Something not a lot of stars could accomplish. Being able to balance love and fame equally. Very few could achieve such feat, but there Jesse was: a lot more accustomed to his new life in the 50s.

Just like Elvis had a group of professional performers, so did Jesse. And his band comprised none other than the original bandmates of Elvis Presley's band. He'd gone out of his way to find them. Finding them proved rather difficult but was even more challenging was convincing them to be his band members, but of course, as though a force was helping him, Jesse had pulled it off and recruited James.

Burton as his lead guitarist, Jerry Scheff; responsible for handling the bass guitar. John Wilkinson saw the rhythm guitar, Ron Tutt, to the drums, with Larry Muhoberac running the keyboard.

Larry and James were both been born in Louisiana, and from the history, he knew about both men, it wasn't until years into the future that they would leave to explore more musical grounds and pursue their musical career. That was why he'd gone ahead to find them. He knew that some of the band members lived longer than most and some didn't.

He found it amazing that he knew how the lives of some of these people would turn out to be like. History was playing out the way it was supposed to for some, but for those whose lives Jesse was in was different. He was somehow altering history, and he wasn't sure what the consequences were, but it'd been good so far. Life was good.

One of the perks that came with being a true fanatic of someone was that you knew almost everything you could about them. Before he'd left, he learned to actualize his plan; he needed to know more about the people whose presence was of vital essence to his idol.

Although he didn't do it alone—he had help from Sam and having to explain the need to recruit specific people had been rather tasking, seeing that he needed to be convincing. But Sam trusted his judgment, and though he didn't know why Jesse insisted on Elvis' band members, he didn't ask questions. Since he first met Jesse, he'd been that way, and he noticed that whatever the boy said usually turned out to be true. To Sam, the young man was a mystery.

It was mainly because of this that Sam always helped Jesse whenever he needed it.

The man had somehow figured that asking Jesse questions were pointless. He never spoke about his personal life to anyone. And Sam didn't ask questions. As long as whatever Jesse didn't jeopardize his future as a rising star and the record label, he was good.

Jesse was all about secrecy, but he made sure not to bother those around him. He'd managed that at least. Even as a young child.

Maybe it was because that was his true purpose of living, or perhaps it was due to something else but, he realized he still knew a lot about Elvis than he remembered about certain other things he should have.

The band members were mostly very young. So, convincing them that the life they were living could be a lot better if they could only leave the only home they'd known for so long took a lot of effort. Jesse had to share his own story of leaving behind the most important person in his life to be where he was.

They were all men, so they understood what it meant. Jesse had told Ron that he didn't have to abandon his family.

He explained to the young boy that he allowed him to be someone for himself and help his family. Not that his family was doing poorly, but as a man, it was his duty to.

Jesse had told Ron he could leave if he wanted, but he told him he hoped he'd give the music life a try first. If what he was offered wasn't what he wanted, then he could move on to find greener pastures.

As for Jerry Scheff and John Wilkinson phoned both men at first and even offered to pay to come to pick them up himself. It was a challenging feat to achieve— bringing them all together, but he did it nonetheless.

For months, they trained together. In the long run, they all became more than just bandmates, and they became friends. Good ones.

As time went on, Jesse Stockholm released some songs. The songs became popular, and because of this, Jesse became sought-out. Along with his band members and, of course, Sam Phillips as the founder of the record label Jesse was signed under.

He was nervous. Requests came in now and then asking him to perform live on stages. Jesse had his band ready on standby, but he was a nervous wreck.

He knew he'd performed on stage when he was still a little boy. Back when his father was *his father*. He realized he didn't remember much about his childhood. It was as though the more he grew accustomed to life in the time he was, memories of his life from *the future* were slowly fading.

✶✶✶

"Yes, buttercup. I remember that we made plans for dinner tonight. And I promised to be there, didn't I?" The boys were in the studio having to practice as usual when the telephone rang. Ron had been the one to pick, and he'd handed the phone to Jesse when the caller said she wanted to talk to her boyfriend.

The band members chuckled in the corner. "*Yes, buttercup,*" James mimicked. The rest of the boys burst out laughing.

Jesse pretended not to hear.

Amongst the six of them, he was the only one with a girlfriend. It wasn't due to any privileges as the star boy of the group; it just happened to be that way. That's why his band-turned-friends never missed the opportunity to tease him. These boys were living vicariously through him in matters of love, and they loved every moment of it.

They had a live performance coming up in a few weeks, and they'd been going at it in the studio for quite some time now.

"I love you too. See you after practice." Ron waited for Jesse to drop the phone before doing a loud drumroll while the other boys cheered him on. The studio was filled with laughter, clapping, and salutes. "Gentlemen, give it up for our favorite star and friend, Jesse Stockholm. Lover to Dorothy and star boy to the whole of Memphis." John's joke had everyone laughing. Even Jesse joined in.

Jesse shook his head, smiling. "Oh, shut up, John. You'll see who's going to be laughing next when you snag yourself a woman. It's a promise." He pointed his right index finger to his chest. "So, believe me when I say, it's gonna be me."

They were still laughing when Sam came in. "Boys, everything good? You're not having any problems, right?" They all chimed in. "No, Sam."

"Yeah, we're good. Except that these boys here are without women, and they're just jealous. Can you believe that, Sam?" Jesse smirked. His grin widened when he caught Larry roll his eyes. They'd gotten so close. Jesse now saw them as more than friends. They were like the brothers he never had. Now and then, during practice, they'd make a joke or two. There was seldom a dull moment whenever they got together. And even outside of training, they were close.

Sometimes they made plans to hang out together. It was something Jesse suggested. A way for them to bond and have a real relationship and not just one based on the fact that they were in the same music group.

The others thought it wasn't such a bad idea, and since then, they hung out whenever they could. Although there were times when one or two band members were absent, they never let it affect anything. The ones absent consistently caught up to whatever gist they missed. In this case, Larry was constantly updating them on how he loved to poke fun at the others.

So, Jesse seeing his reaction made him crack a smile. Sam shook his head. He raised his hand as though telling him to come off it.

"Okay. Are you all set to begin?" Sam was a very disciplined man. Though he was playful with the boys, he was just as strict and severe in matters related to business. And maybe that was why people sought him out. He handled the Sun Records label so well that not only did it show in the kind of people he signed, but also the kind of people who sought him out. Other producers always wanted to work with him.

Sam Phillips was the kind of person who knew how to play his cards right. He was confident in himself, and he had a very keen sense of judgment.

When some of the other producers Sam worked what been against Jesse's decision to bring the band in, he'd been the only one who agreed. And somehow, when the other producers saw this, they gave in as well.

Jesse had been so shocked by it. It was then he knew that to work with Sam Phillips had to one of the best privileges he'd ever been gifted. This man as a person and not just his name; had influence. Jesse knew he'd made the right decision coming here.

Ron responded with a drum roll. "Alright."

Sam made to leave but came back, "I know you're all working hard, and I appreciate your efforts. Be rest assured I see all you do, boys. Your efforts don't go unnoticed." He put his hands in his pocket and continued, "And I know you're wondering how I know, seeing that I'm almost always not around. Just know that I see you all. Alright?"

"Alright, Sam."

"Good." Sam nodded, satisfied. "Now, about the show. It's around the corner, and I won't be around for the next one week, but I know you'll all do fine on your own till then. But I'll be back in time for the show. You have all you need, and if you need me, you know how to reach me."

The boys nodded in unison.

They had a pre-show that evening. Sam had made sure to invite all those he could. The boys did too. It was something Sam suggested they do. He wanted to know what their shortcomings were. He'd gotten both producers and non-producers. Sam wanted judgment both from a professional point of view and that of an audience. The man wasn't a perfectionist, but he was close. He was doing what was best for the label and those who it comprised.

"I'll be here until after today's pre-show. Good luck." He waved after his speech and left without waiting for a reply.

Larry spoke up. His hands pressed down on the keyboard as he talked. "You know, sometimes I wonder he's the same person." He switched to a C scale. "One minute, he's nice and accommodating, and the next, he's like a rude boss."

Jesse chuckled. "Oh yeah? And what are you?"

"Rest, will you?"

"NO." Jesse's eyes twinkled. These boys had somehow wormed their way to his heart. They'd made a home, thereby weaving a web, and Jesse was helpless. His affection for them was fierce. He enjoyed teasing them and being teased by them in return.

Jesse felt guilty. As he grew to love these new people in his life, he gradually forgot the ones from *his past.*

He was slowly losing touch with who he was before. The pitiful little boy whose daddy wasn't present for most of his life and was too sad because he couldn't comfort his mother, and he didn't believe he was good enough to. So, he'd run. It ran as an excuse to prove his dad wrong. At least it was what he told himself, and he continued to.

He felt guilty thinking of his mother. He couldn't even remember most of their time together. His dad was out of the question. It's not like he had much with the man anyway.

Rosetta. Man, how he missed her. But these feelings only came to him suddenly. Sometimes he'd find himself doing something; singing, for example, and out of the blues, he'd randomly remember his loved ones.

If he was honest, he didn't run from anyone but himself. He knew if his dad was always present in his life, he knew that if his father had chosen family over work, chosen to be with them instead— he would not have gone. He would never have left his poor mother behind.

It was selfish of him. He knew that. Selfish to have wanted more when he had all he needed, but then again, he didn't. He wanted a father. A family. He'd wished his family would be whole again. That was all he'd ever wanted. That was his one true wish. If he'd gotten that, if his father had just acknowledged him when he wanted it the most, he wouldn't be here.

Even now, he craved his father. He wanted him to see the man he was slowly becoming: his mom too, and Rosetta.

But even with everything that happened, Jesse was happy with his new life. Maybe not satisfied, but he felt proud of himself for making it this far and achieving what he set out to. Even Lisa *Reed* would be proud of him.

Jesse didn't even hear his friends murmuring in the background. He was far gone with his thoughts to pay them any heed.

"He's doing that thing again. That thing when he just completely blanks out." Ron tried to whisper as lightly as he could. His friends always noticed when it happened, but neither of them had asked him about it.

They never told him, but when they first arrived, Sam called each of them and separately spoke to them about Jesse.

Sam never told them why, but he'd told them not to ask questions, and they complied.

But it was getting out of hand, and James couldn't take it any longer. They weren't just bandmates anymore; they'd fast become something more substantial, and acting like nothing was happening was eating at him.

It wasn't just about respecting his privacy anymore. Whatever it was, he was confident it was terrible. What, with the way he always randomly zoned out on them, it'd have to take a mad person, not ask.

James took a step towards his friend. He touched his shoulder lightly. "Jesse, what's wrong? You keep zoning out now and then."

"I- fuck." Jesse ran his palms down his face. *How long did I zone out?* He forced a smile. "I'm good, bro. I promise."

Neither James nor the others bought the lie, but they had pressing matters to attend to. Whatever it was, if he wasn't going to talk about it immediately, then they were sure it could wait.

CHAPTER 10

"We all know this day isn't complete without our star boy giving us something." The MC— a middle-aged-looking man spoke into the mic. "So please, ladies and gentlemen, let's give it up for JESSE STOCKHOLM and the TCB band!"

There was an immediate uproar from the crowd. Jesse emerged backstage, a mic already set on stage waiting for him, band members in tow. The drums had been earlier arranged ahead of the performance. Jerry, John, and James all had their guitars strapped across their bodies. The piano also sat in wait on stage.

They all waved to the crowd, smiling.

"Jesseeeeee!"

"I love you, Jesse Stockholm!"

"Stockholm! Stockholm!! Stockholm!!!"

The crowd cheered him on from every corner. Both men and women alike. However, there were more women than men. Jesse had risen to stardom, setting a name for himself.

Ever since the first appearance at the preshow, Jesse and his band, which he'd given the same original name to— *taking care of business*, they'd all been working hard. As he promised, Sam

Phillips had been present for the preshow and came back in time to present at their first live concerts.

After months of working diligently and relentlessly on an album with his band and producer, Jesse released his first album. And just like his idol, he titled it *Jesse Stockholm Rock n' Roll*.

Many had gone crazy with love at the release of the new album. Jesse had put a lot into it. So, when he received the reaction from the audience and reviews from producers and other music experts, he'd felt elated. It pushed him to do more. To want to work even more challenging. And he did.

Now here he was, on a stage with his band in front of thousands of people screaming their lungs out. They loved him, and he knew it. He loved the feeling it gave me, the sense of fulfillment and satisfaction.

The cheering continued. The crowd chanted Jesse's and the band's names.

"TCB, Wooоahhhhh!"

Jesse held on to the microphone; he started slowly, bending as though he was squatting—slowly standing upright, "Hellllooooo Memphis!" Again, the crowd cheered. Even louder this time. He smiled brightly at the audience in front of him. He'd done it.

The stage was in an open arena, so the screams of people could be heard from afar. It even attracted more people. Sam had suggested they use the venue instead of a closed theatre. The first group of tickets had all been sold out, yet he made preparations for more. As if he had predicted the outcome of the concert.

Even as Jesse and his band stood, some staff members were selling tickets outside to the newcomers. Everyone wanted to be a witness to their performance.

"Okay, so, here's what we're going to do. I'll sing a special one for you, but I want you to sing along with me in the rest. Okay, Memphis?"

The people cheered in response. He'd noticed one common thing amongst people here. Whenever there was a concert, most of them never really sang along. Leaving it all to the artist, he didn't know why but felt that wasn't how it was supposed to be.

He turned his attention to his band, signaling them to start. "I'm thrilled to be here, and I hope you are too."

He wakes up in the morning, and the song started in a low tone

Does his teeth bite to eat, and he's rolling

Never changes a thing

The weekends the week begins

She thinks we look at each other

Wondering what the other is thinking

But we never say a thing

These crimes between us grow deeper…

He sang the lyrics passionately, one particular woman on his mind the entire time. His beautiful Dorothy. How he'd grown to love her, they'd been courting for a year now, and not a single day went past without him loving her more. She reminded him greatly of someone important in his life, but there were times he didn't even remember who.

Dorothy had become the most important person in his life. And his friends had become his best guys. At that point, he wanted nothing more.

He continued to sing the lyrics, his mind filled with nothing but love at the people who stood in front of him.

Take these chances

Place them in a box until a quieter time

Lights down, you up and die.

They were going to perform Shake, Rattle, and Roll next.

Band member James opened the song. His right hand was placed lightly on the fingerboard as his fingers struck the strings of the guitar. His left hand down at the body also struck chords of their own. John and Jerry also chimed in on their turn, with Larry on the keyboard and Ron on the drums. They played with all their heart.

Well, get out of that bed, wash your face and hands

Get out of that bed, wash your face and hands

Well, get in that kitchen, make some noise with the pots and pans.

I believe it in my soul; you're the devil in nylon hose

I believe it in my soul; you're the devil in nylon hose

The harder I work, the faster my money goes

Jesse dragged his left leg from side to side while he took short strides with the right—Elvis Presley's signature hip dance. Jesse performed it there on stage. His action elicited shouts from the women in the crowd. He sang his heart out, just as he had practiced.

Well, I said-

Shake, rattle, and roll, the crowd sang along.

I said-

Shake, rattle, and roll

I said shake, rattle, and roll

I said-

Shake, rattle and roll. He put his hands behind his head, thrusting his hips forward flexibly. His energy was wild, and people clapped in turn. He went crazy with adrenaline; his power was remarkable that even his bandmates seemed surprised.

They did a couple of songs, entertaining almost all of Memphis.

※※※

"I'm telling you, Sam, if you don't keep him under control, you'll regret it. Do you see the way he dances, and goodness, why does he always wear shirts like that?" One of the producers Sam was close to, Joe, thought that Jesse's dancing was too dirty and the deep neck Jesse had started wearing wasn't good for the image of the record label.

The subject of the topic felt otherwise. However, there was a backlash from the press, with him making it the tabloids. A lot of people questioned not only his dancing at performances but also his style of fashion.

He'd been wearing a lot of deep necks and showing off his flexibility and agility through his dance moves. Amidst the backlash from the press, producers, and generally, those from the music industry, Jesse brought nothing but fame, success, and sound money to Sun Records.

His fans kept him going; they pushed him to want to do more, which he did. At first, his fans talked, some even complained that his dance was inappropriate, but they got to love it with them. It became a trend that everyone wanted to copy.

But even those who copied it couldn't pull it off as he did. *No one does it like Jesse Stockholm.*

Things were going relatively well for Jesse and his bandmates, as well as the record label he was signed to. Such that, even Sam Phillips had left him to do as he pleased. So long as he was bringing sales to the company. Sam knew that though he might wild on stage and came off as someone with a rather weird style of dressing, he never tried anything that would jeopardize the company's image.

Jesse had spoken to Sam one on one when news about him had been speculating, he'd promised Sam that no matter what happened, he would never put the company's name in danger, and he was doing a great job on keeping his promise.

✲✲✲

To those around Jesse Stockholm, the very ones who were involved in his life, Jesse came off as someone always happy. He rarely had simple problems in his life. And when he issues, they were seldom too conflicting.

That wasn't the case, though. Jesse's problems were not the everyday kind of problems. He was slowly losing a sense of who he was and where he came from. He couldn't remember the faces and names of people from his *past*. Goodness, even his mother. Once, he almost forgot her name, but he'd been quick to write it down in a journal he kept away from prying eyes.

Her face, had it not been due to some pictures he kept with him, he'd have completely forgotten what she looked like.

As for his father, Liam Stockholm, it had been a relatively long time he had thought of the man. Though he owed it to him the man, he was today. Still, he had a significant catalyst in making him the man who didn't want to leave his mother behind.

He always hated how guilty he felt whenever he tried to remember the names and faces; he was supposed to but couldn't.

Rosetta, dear him. He had completely forgotten what she looked like. He never took pictures of the maid, nor did he ever really ask her for one. He only ever had his mother's photos. The more he grew accustomed to his life in Memphis, the less he remembered life from the time he came from.

No one noticed how lonely he felt sometimes; Jesse did an excellent job at concealing his emotions. Especially the kind he didn't want people knowing about.

Since the first performance on stage, he'd been getting many offers from other producers who wanted to work with him.

He'd been to a lot of interviews. He went alone. Some he went with his producer, Sam Phillips, and others he had with his band. People wanted him to make an appearance in their shows and even songs. Some he turned down, some he agreed to, and some he regretted accepting.

Most interviewers, shows, or reporters asked him a common question, and he always never answered. They all wanted to know where he was from, who his father and mother were if he had any siblings. And when someone had asked why he always evaded the question, his reply had been he fell out with dad when he was younger, and he had lived with his mom for some time before he left.

Jesse had mainly forgotten about his childhood, so he'd created a story in his head about what happened when he was younger, and when they'd asked about the whereabouts of his family, he gave a vague response. *They're home.* The bigger question was, *where was this home he spoke of?*

Sam Phillips himself, together with the members of Taking Care of Business, had grown quite curious themselves. At first, Larry speculated to the other members that Sam wouldn't have hired a total stranger.

Larry believed Sam at least knew Jesse's hometown, but the boys found out that wasn't the case. Neither of them probed for answers, however.

Jesse worried for himself. He suspected that a find would come when he would forget his family, but before he did, he wanted to share that part of himself with his woman, Dorothy. He felt guilty for keeping it from her all this time, but he was finally ready to tell her.

He felt that if there was someone from the 50s who knew his identity, then it should be someone whom he saw as his equal and the one genuine person he loved with everything he had and wanted to share everything with. His one and only, Dorothy. He hated keeping things from her. Jesse had never kept anything from her. Except, of course, where he came from.

He resolved to tell her the truth.

✳✳✳

"I know it's hard to believe, but it's the truth, baby." Jesse was feeling very nervous. He shifted his feet uncomfortably before he continued. "And the rumors about me falling from the sky isn't exactly a lie. I'm from the future." *I'm from the future?* Even a mad man would think he was crazy.

Dorothy said nothing, she just stared at him, waiting for him to break, but he didn't. He kept a straight face throughout the entire conversation. And then she laughed.

Of course. What was I thinking? That she'd believe something like that? Who would? He rubbed his palm across his stubble in frustration. His facial hairs had decided to show themselves some months back.

'Look, Dolly, this is not a joke." He usually used her pet's name whenever he was sweet, but this time was the opposite. Jesse was as serious as a heart attack, but she didn't know that. Come with me. I'll show you. He stood, leading the way to his bedroom. Dorothy followed behind.

His gut told him that it wasn't too late to stop, to play along and say it was a joke after all, but he couldn't. He didn't want to hide the truth from her anymore. She deserved to know.

He squatted down and stretched as far as he could. There was shuffling under the bed, but he finally found what he was looking for. His bag. The one he'd brought with him when he first arrived. It was dusty from the absence of touch.

He unzipped it and peeked inside the bag. Jesse rummaged through the pack, looking for something in particular. Dorothy stood at a corner, curiosity getting the best of her. She tipped her head to the side, trying to look at the contents of the bag.

First, there was a clatter, followed by ruffling. Suddenly, Jesse stopped. "Found it!"

See, look here. He beckoned her to come closer. Look at what it says, "*this is my new present. I am now Jesse Stockholm, a teenager in the early 1950s.*" His girlfriend had nothing but confusion written all over her face. She sighed. "This doesn't exactly prove anything, Jesse. It's a paper with words written on it. You can stop it now; I know you're joking."

He ran his hands through his hair. They were long with his bangs hanging at the front. Just the way Elvis liked to keep his. *This isn't enough proof.* He picked the bag up again. If she didn't believe the note, she would believe him when she saw the rest.

So, he brought out his phone, the charger, and his MP3 player. One that contained all of Elvis Presley's songs, along with the photos of his mom. Both the ones of her alone and both of them together. He raised them, almost shoving them in her face. "See!"

Dorothy's pupils widened like hundred millimeters more. She was utterly astonished. "What are these?" She took a step back. "Jesse, what do you have in your hands."

"The truth." His eyes begged her. "I don't want to hide this from you any longer. You're my woman Dolly, and you deserve to know everything about me. Especially since you're the only woman, I see a future with you.

He took a step forward. Dorothy went rigid. He dropped the gadgets on the bed and held up the photos. "This is my mom, and that's me next to her, Dolly. My mother. She's the one. The same one you've been asking to meet. Unfortunately, it's not possible, and I swear, I wish it was. I wouldn't want to take anyone else, but you home to my mama." He meant every word he said, even though they were all told in a moment of desperation.

He knelt. "I'm truly sorry for keeping this from you for so long. I should have said something earlier when you asked, and not just told you to trust me. I could have been frank with you from the start, and I'm genuinely sorry.

"Please. I love you."

Dorothy's heart broke seeing him kneeling on the floor, begging for her forgiveness, for her understanding. But she was too overwhelmed by all of it. The truth— she couldn't come to terms with it yet. She found it hard to process any of it. If what he said was true, then- then- he wasn't from here.

The blonde woman had so many thoughts running through her head at that moment. Why did he come here then? If he was from the future, then a lot of things had changed. It was evident from the technology he showed her earlier. She wasn't even sure what they could do, and she was too scared to find out.

All this time, all this while, she'd been in love with a man from an entirely different space and time.

Jesse was scared. He wasn't sure he'd ever been this scared in his entire life, and even if he was, he couldn't remember. Dorothy had been mute since he'd come clean. He wasn't sure what to do or say. He wasn't sure about anything, and it scared him to the bones. *Should I not have said anything? No! It's good I did. No more lies or secrecy.* Besides, he'd carried the weight of his identity on his shoulder for so long. He wasn't sure he could anymore.

Fuck, he hadn't even told her everything yet, but he wasn't even sure what it was that was missing. He wanted to say to her about his childhood, who his mother was, and where she was from. What she liked and disliked. How she spoke, the sound of her voice.

And his dad, he wanted to tell her who his father was, but he couldn't even remember much. Memories of his former self were almost gone. He was sure he wanted to tell her more, but he didn't know where to begin. No, he couldn't remember where to begin.

He feared he would soon forget his purpose. The real reason he went back in time in the first place. The real reason why he was where he was. Most of all, he feared he would lose his lover. She meant so much to him than he'd even realized. It wasn't until he was on his knees begging her to stay that he realized just how much this woman had come to mean to him.

Jesse wanted to spend the rest of his life with her and grow old with her. He wanted her to have his kids, but Jesse wasn't sure he could have that anymore. Not with the way she was looking at him.

"Dolly, please say something." He couldn't stand her silence. It was eating at him. It made him nervous and scared. He couldn't lose her. He didn't want to. "I love you, please." But she shook her head. And just like that, she backed away from him slowly. He stood, his hands stretched out, calling for her. "Please, don't go. Don't leave me, please." Jesse Stockholm's heart shattered to a billion pieces. *No! Fuck, no!*

If there indeed were a god-like people claimed, then he wouldn't let him lose the love of his life. There was only so much he could take, and losing Dorothy wasn't on the menu.

As fast as she could, she bolted for the door, leaving him chasing after her. She didn't stop. Not for anyone or him, for that matter.

❋❋❋

Weeks passed without Dorothy in his life anymore. Slowly, he started drinking till it became a habit. He would drink before and after every show. He would drown himself in alcohol, go to pubs for the women, and whatever else the places offered. He was in pain, and the only way he saw to go about it was to drink himself to stupor.

Everyone around him was worried. His friends had even tried to get in touch with his ex-girlfriend, but they couldn't. It was like she had just vanished. No one knew where she went, and those who did refuse to say a word.

Jesse was slowly turning into everything he wasn't, and it was only a matter of time before he ruined everything. He started to make things difficult for everyone.

CHAPTER 11

"It wasn't supposed to be like this! None of this was meant to happen!" Jesse grabbed a handful of his hair. He was frustrated. He sat on a leather footstool. There was a round vanity mirror in his room. He's gotten it for a reason, and the said reason wasn't even present-Dorothy.

Along with it, he'd bought a fine wooden dressing table. He wanted his Dolly to sit in front of it while she did her best to look for him. That was impossible now.

Since the day he told her about who he was and where he was from, since the moment she walked out of his apartment, he hadn't heard from her. He had gone looking that day and several other days, but it had been fruitless. *She wouldn't leave me. She wouldn't-*, countless times, he had tried to reassure himself, but Jesse wasn't sure what to believe anymore.

Jesse's life was at a standstill. He knew it, and so did his friends and producer. They all witnessed Jesse slip into a terrible state of depression. At first, they thought it was because of Dorothy, but they realized it was something more with time, but neither of them could ask what. Instead, they'd stopped asking. He never shared his problems with anyone.

There were moments his friends would come around to keep him company. Larry, the funny one of the groups, told jokes at every opportunity he got. All to make Jesse feel less sadness. Even in those moments, Jesse wanted nothing more but to cry. He and the band could be having a good time, yet the thoughts that raced through his mind were how alone he felt.

Even now, as Jesse sat on the stool, he wanted to curl himself up into a fetal position and cry in his mother's arms, but he knew he never could. *I can't go home, nor can I cry and feel better.*

He chuckled bitterly. *All I feel is sadness. And maybe dad was right, and I could never be Elvis Presley. What did you think, huh? That you could bolt to the past and steal someone else's life and be happy?* He let out a pained laugh. *Of course, leaving your mother behind in pursuit of what? Happiness? Approval? Or were you just looking for an excuse?*

He knew he was right. Jesse wasn't even sure why he left anymore. To prove himself right or his father wrong. What did it matter, though? In the end, he was the one feeling miserable, and he couldn't even go back. And no matter how much the fantastic people in his life tried to make him feel better, to show that they were there for him, and tried to spend time with him. But Jesse knew his worry couldn't be easily soothed.

No one would truly understand him. He did try explaining to someone once, and what happened? She left him. He ran as though he was venomous. Jesse knew that no matter how much he tried to dissuade himself from feeling less than he already did, it was pointless.

Jesse knew that even if he tried getting others to understand just to see if anyone truly got him, he knew that no matter the possibility of him telling them how he felt, no one could understand him but *himself*. So, he didn't bother. He never tried but kept everything locked up.

He had to get to the studio in thirty minutes. Earlier in the morning, he'd received a call from the company. It was Sam. He told Jesse he needed him at the studio to complete the song he was working on earlier with James Burton, one of the band members. He let out a sigh. If he was to get there on time, he best get to it.

The wooden wardrobe stood adjacent to the vanity. It had three sections with inner sections to it. He dreaded opening it, just as he had since it dawned on him his Dorothy wasn't coming back. Her clothes were still there. He'd let her use one section, but it wasn't enough. So, she had started using his area.

He liked how it made him feel then, knowing he shared something with her. But now, though the house was empty, her presence remained. She did a number on him.

As quickly as he could, he got dressed. He'd wasted enough time reminiscing on the woman who walked out of his life. Sam wouldn't take it lightly should he arrive late.

He fished out a pair of black pants from his wardrobe and a checkered button-up short-sleeved shirt. He wore his favorite pair of white stockings with black shoes. He tucked the shirt in his trousers and hastily grabbed a cap from his drawer. Jesse was set to go. *I'll take the red Chevrolet.*

✸✸✸

Sam was sitting in his office; his raven hair looked a bit longer since Jesse last saw him.

"Good day, Sam." Jesse paused; Sam was on the phone with someone. Star boy Jesse took a stroll to the far end of the wall. Hands in pocket as he waited for Sam to get off the phone.

"Yeah, I just need a black one. The one I got seems to be broken." Jesse wasn't sure what he was talking about, and he wasn't interested in finding out what it was.

Jesse blacked him out. He wrote many songs recently, but it turned out that he couldn't bring himself to release them. Some he'd written alone, and some he'd been corresponding with James. The boy was a good songwriter, almost as good as Jesse.

At the moment, they were both working on one, but something was missing. He and James had decided to take some time off to find inspiration. It seemed like James had gotten his. If not, Sam wouldn't have called him the studio. Though he knew James would have told him first, Sam had probably been on the young man's neck that he'd told him, yes, to get him off. Sam was that persistent. Wanting to make sure everything was done correctly, and since he saw the last song he and James wrote, he'd been keeping tabs on them both. Technically on James, because Jesse wasn't in the right state of mind to entertain any of Sam's disturbances.

Jesse looked at Sam; he was still going on about who knows what. He wanted to get away from the office to think. He signaled to Sam that he would be in the studio. Hands in pocket, Jesse walked off, wondering of a good excuse to get away for a short time. *Maybe a vacation somewhere would nice.* But where? He tried to think of some places he could visit.

Maybe-

The studio was empty. *What?* There was no James, nor was there any other member of the Taking Care of Business band. Just then, Sam came in. *Great timing, Sam.* He had a white envelope in his right hand.

"Have a seat, Jesse. We need to discuss the content of this letter." The hairs on Jesse's body stood as his body sank into one of the sofas. *What could it possibly be?*

"As you can see, James isn't here. I called you before I called him." Sam continued. "Else, I'd have waited for when you come in tomorrow to give it to you." Jesse wondered if Dorothy has finally written him. For a moment, he got nervous and excited. Sam noticed it. He knew exactly what Jesse was thinking.

"Wait, I'll stop you right there." His hand was raised. "It's not from who you think it is. Dorothy, right?" Sam's expression was one of pity. His face softened as he reached out to pat Jesse on the shoulder. "Anyway, you've been called to serve your country. You got drafted, boy."

The army. Of late, he'd only been writing songs to get his mind off things; he'd written so many but hadn't released any of them. And now, news that he got called to the army? Jesse chuckled. "What a day." The timing couldn't have been more perfect. He smiled close-mouthed. *Great!*

His producer looked at him. Jesse was one particular young man. Just a while ago, he didn't seem too happy knowing the letter wasn't the sender he thought it was, and now he knew where it was from, he seemed rather pleased.

Sam Phillips had thought he would take the news differently, but the boy had he been wrong. All letters sent to Jesse's had been coming to his house. Jesse hadn't changed the address since he moved out, so Sam got them instead and brought them to him at the studio. Not that he received much anyway. Most of the letters admirers or fans wrote to him were delivered straight to the studio.

"I take it from the expression on your face that my job here is done." Jesse's producer stood up and made his way out, not even bothering to wait for a reply. The young singer shook his head after him, smiling. Sam was one helluva character.

✱✱✱

Jesse, along with some other young men who were also enrolled in the military, stood at the train station. They all stared at him. Mainly because they couldn't believe that *Jesse Stockholm* was also going to the army, but in all honestly, it's not like he could refuse. Sam had randomly brought it up, but Jesse didn't pay mind. He figured when the time came. He would cross that bridge.

He owed a lot to Sam, especially since he mostly had no proof of citizenship. Sam had taken care of it without asking too many questions. He was, after all, from a different time. Which was why he couldn't bring himself to say no when his producer suggested he enroll.

Now here he was, in a train station waiting for a train that would take him to his assigned bunker.

✱✱✱

The journey was as he expected, the young men on the train looking at him like one would a superstar. Some even asked for his autograph. Some were too shocked to speak. One time during the ride, some of the guys introduced themselves. No one asked him cause they all knew who he was. So, he decided to ask one of the guys sitting next to him, but the guy had been too shocked to speak.

They arrived in camp after some time on the road. He hoped to be treated like every other person.

Jesse didn't want any unique treatments but that hard. Even on his arrival, some senior officers called him aside and told him they could assign him to a different room just for himself. He refused. For one, he didn't want special attention, nor did he want to be alone in his room. He tried to get along with the other cadets.

It seemed tempting. First, he knew that though the celebrity lifestyle wasn't what he wanted, he was used to living in luxury. Even before he got to Memphis, his dad was a multi-millionaire scientist after all, and though the man wasn't present in his life, he and his mom lacked nothing.

The beds were small, and they weren't allowed to use their phones. Being there meant being deprived of a lot of things. He wasn't sure how long he could last. Maybe he should have said yes to that particular treatment request.

The first few weeks were hard for Jesse. He found it hard adjusting to life in the military. He might have a friendly, flexible, and strong body, but the army was on a different level. He wasn't physically fit for most of the activities going on in camp. It didn't help that some of his fellow cadets didn't take him seriously. They saw him as a privileged person who wasn't serious. He hated it.

He spent extra time alone trying to do better. He got help from some other cadets he'd befriended. He was terrible at most of the pieces of training, but gradually, he got better.

Jesse also made sure to get paid the same thirty-five dollars as his fellow cadets. He'd been offered more at first, of course, and he could have accepted, but he had enough money. More than enough. But mostly, he wanted to be treated equally like the others.

Finally, after so much effort, Jesse adapted fully to life in the camp. His cadets treated him equally, and so did the lieutenants and colonels. There were times people forgot and tried to treat him differently, but he always refused. He earned the respect of his cadets and senior officers.

With his new adaption came a personal change for Jesse. He decided to go by his middle name. His cadets and seniors questioned his decision, and he told them that life in the military opened his eyes to a lot he never knew. If he was going to drop the fame, he might as well drop the name.

It took a lot of remembering from his mates and a lot of getting used to for Jesse, but the name Ben eventually stuck.

Time flew by. Ben spent a lot of his free time writing songs. He created a lot of lyrics about his lost love, Dorothy. His mother. The cadets and friends lost in battle. He realized that camp training was nothing compared to the actual war out there, and he was lucky to be one of the few who always made it back.

He spoke to his bandmates now and then. Also, to Sam, his producer. They always had something new to tell him, and he was always glad to relay his experience in the army to them. They found it fascinating.

The best part of his days in camp was when letters came in from Dorothy. Somehow, she'd heard about his enrolment and decided to write to him. They both exchanged letters. He told her how he'd decided to go by his middle name, but she still called him Jesse. He apologized for hiding the truth from her for so long, and Dorothy being the sweetheart she was, forgave him.

Ben told her of the new songs he wrote, told her of his experiences at concerts. He had so much to say to her, and he couldn't always do so in the letters. He told her of the battles, of the cadets who he'd become close with, and even some of the senior officers.

He told her of the rigorous practices, of the songs and the nicknames. He told her of everything he could, and most importantly, he never failed to tell her how much he loved her. She did the same. Dorothy told him how she often went back to his apartment to feel his presence or feel connected to him.

Ben couldn't wait to leave camp. His sweetheart had shared so much with the back-and-forth letters. And clearly, the tension between them had grown. He wanted to do more than just hold her in his arms.

✳✳✳

Finally, the day I've been waiting for. Ben's friends from the band, many of his fans, and Sam Phillips were at the train station to pick him up. Sadly, his darling Dorothy wasn't.

Everyone was happy to have him back. They threw a party on his behalf. And if he was honest, it felt good to be back. He'd told his closest friends about his name change, but many of his still called him Jesse. He did, however, tell them about it.

Ben was having the party of the month. He was happy, but nothing prepared him for the news that came after.

His Dorothy, his darling. The love of his life was gone. And just like that, everything he'd worked hard to achieve went down the drain. He learned that she was sick, and she died a few days before his return.

Ben was devastated. What would he do without her gone? It was funny how he'd been the one to leave the most influential persons in his life only to be rejected by the next most important person to him. Ben rapidly slipped into depression, and this time, no matter what anyone did it tried to do, they couldn't help him.

Stockholm couldn't help but blame himself for her death. If only he hadn't enrolled. If only he hadn't hidden the truth from her. She wouldn't have left, and they would have been together. He could have taken care of her.

Ben wanted nothing more than to bring her back. Back to him, where she belonged.

CHAPTER 12

The loss of Dorothy was still something Ben was struggling with. It had been two months since he'd gotten the news. The hurt was still too fresh. Time they say, "heals everything." But Stockholm knew it wasn't true. Instead, he knew a time would come where he wouldn't cry at the sound of her time, nor would his chest hurt at the thought of her. When the sight of something that was once hers wouldn't break his heart, nor his lungs constrict when he saw her face in a picture. He knew he wouldn't stop loving her.

Dorothy was his first love, and it wasn't like they hadn't reconciled. No, they'd even exchanged letters and made plans for when he got out. Of course, he wanted to spend the rest of his life with her, but life had its plans. And from that moment on, it no longer included his Dolly.

Ben wondered if Dorothy knew she would die before he got out. But, asides from her parents, he knew Dorothy better than anyone. And he was certain that even if she knew she could die, she would remain hopeful and praying for a miracle.

He was never religious, yet she never tried to force her religion on him and that he was hopeful for. His Dolly was never the demanding type. Rather, she accepted him for who he was. She would smile and say to him, "you wouldn't be who you are if you didn't have the certain things that made you. You are different because you are *you*, Jesse. If there were another one of you, you wouldn't be special now, would you?"

Amongst many other things, she accepted him for who he was. To his knowledge, she never judged him. Not once when they were together nor after, Dorothy was his confidant in so many matters. She understood him, and when she didn't, she would listen so that she could. She never made impulsive decisions; she was as gentle as a dove—the only one who ever complimented him. Where Ben lacked, she made up for. Unlike two peas in a pod, she was his strength and vice versa.

It didn't take long for Ben to slip into a depressing state. And though it didn't come as a surprise, it nonetheless made those around him worried about him. No one could blame him, though. In the time when Dorothy was alive, she and Ben had been inseparable. But now, she was no more. To Ben, he had lost a better part of himself. However, Dorothy was more than just *a* missing piece, she was irreplaceable and deep down, and he feared he would never love another woman the way he did her.

To Jesse Ben Stockholm, everyone had only one soulmate, be it in this life or the next, or whatever it was life all about. And he had just lost his. Though he wasn't religious, he had his own beliefs.

Sam Phillips, along with his bandmates, tried to help him, but it was fruitless. Even Dorothy's mother came around now and then to see him. His friends had reached out to her seeing there was little they could do to help him.

On some days, Ben would go without eating. So he'd drowned himself in his thoughts that he sometimes forgot what day it was and to get meals. He'd grown thin. His dead lover's mother prepared his favorite dish (Cobb salad) whenever she was coming around.

Ben never refused her meals, and whenever he tried, she would say things like, "I went out of my way to make this for you; Dolly would be sad to see you like this, don't make me mad, Jesse." The older woman was one of the few who still called him Jesse and not Ben. She had claimed that it was a hassle switching from Jesse to Ben, and he never forced her to reconsider.

✳✳✳

Ben Stockholm slowly saw how much effort everyone around him made to return to his old self. He felt guilty for making his loved ones worry, and he also wanted to feel better. He was tired of brooding and being glum all the time. Ben knew if he wanted to be fine, he knew he best start acting like it. *What can I do? What should I do? What haven't I done?*

Ben was taking a walk one fine evening when he suddenly remembered his idol, Elvis Presley. How long had it been since he'd thought of him? Ben wasn't certain, but the thought of him now, he suddenly wanted to make everything right. At least, it was what he told himself. Though he knew he couldn't change things, he could at least do this *for himself.* He wasn't sure why, but he wanted to help Elvis. And so, he decided to make his way into town, to the church Elvis performed in on the next Sunday. The very one they'd first met.

Not that he regretted his actions, but he wanted to do something for his idol. To others, Elvis Presley might be a nobody now, but not to Ben Stockholm. As ordinary as Elvis might seem now, he would forever be the king of rock and roll. If not to anyone from this time, to Ben, he was. No one could take one's destiny away from them. It could be delayed but not taken away, and Ben made it a promise to help him realize that destiny. As a key factor to the delay, he was going to set things straight.

✳✳✳

Sunday finally came, and Ben made his way to the Assembly of God's Church. Assemblies of God's Church. He went dressed in his military uniform rather than his usual Jesse Stockholm signature look; a deep neck shirt and a pair of pants. He had long cut his hair short, and even after he got back from camp, he'd kept his hair low — a feature of the new person he wanted to be as Ben.

As he approached the inner building, he heard loud singing from the church. It was a woman. Her voice was soothing yet strong and commanding. Somehow, it made me sad. The lyrics, coupled with the voice, brought sad memories once again.

He noticed that few people recognized who he was. And he was happy about that. He wasn't ready for any meet and chat whatsoever. Very few persons stopped him on his way. Maybe it was the beards or the hair-cut, whichever one, Ben was grateful for it.

He removed his cap and held it in his hand. Though he didn't identify as a Christian or a religious man for that matter, he respected the opinions and ideas of others, and that included religious stands and norms.

He stayed for the service, hoping he would see Elvis, but he didn't. Instead, he saw Gladys Presley, Elvis Presley's mother. He was happy to see the woman. In a way, he felt less bad and more pity towards the woman.

By now, Gladys Presley should have been dead. Had her son, Elvis, become the star he was supporting to be, he would have left her, and the poor woman would have slipped into depression at her only son, leaving abandoning her. But that wasn't the case because Ben had become the star instead. He instantly felt proud of himself. Somehow, he'd prevented such a sad ending for both the woman and her son.

There the older woman was, singing her heart out in front of the congregation. Like her son, she had a beautiful voice. Gladys Presley was alive, but most importantly, she was healthy. Rather than being alive and depressed, she looked content. This brought joy and warmth to Ben's heart.

Seeing Gladys happy made Ben's resolve to help Elvis greater. The smile on her face looked perfect, and he wanted that smile to be on her face for a long time. But, to do that, he needed to aid her son. To get him to a higher level than the one he currently was.

To start, he waited to speak to her after she was done. Ben praised her and told her how much he adored her voice. He even spoke of her son, and his reply when she asked Ben how he knew Elvis had been he'd had an encounter once, and Elvis had been nice to him. She smiled, proud of her son. He went on to ask about his whereabouts; Gladys told him he was working. He spoke to some other people from the church, and they gave him directions and the address of the place. Some were shocked to see him, some too stunned to speak. A few even asked to take a photo with him and get his autograph. It wasn't new to him.

Elvis' place of work was a bit far from the church. Probably an hour and thirty minutes or more to get there on foot and maybe forty-five minutes by car. It was out of town, but he found his way there nonetheless. He took a cab.

Ben made his way to the entrance of the theatre. A lot of people recognized him the moment he walked in. It took him a while to detach himself from the crowd that had gathered around him, but in the end, he was successful.

The star made his way to one of the staff to confirm if Elvis worked there, and the answer was positive. He was just in time. A batch of people had just come out of the movie room after seeing a movie. Meaning the place had to be swept clean for the next group. He had time to converse with Presley before the next movie.

The worker led Ben to where Elvis was. Ben thanked the young man and went in.

He was nervous. Frantically, he rubbed his palms against his jeans. Ironically, Ben was the star here, yet he was the nervous one. Suppose someone knew why they'd laugh and call him crazy. Elvis might be an ordinary theatre worker who liked to sing in church, but Ben knew he wasn't just any man. He was Elvis Aaron Presley. His idol. His star. His role model. Of course, Elvis didn't know that. No one there really did.

At first, Elvis didn't notice Ben, but eventually, he did after Ben cleared his throat.

Ben noticed the expression on Elvis' face. It was one of confusion and shock at the same time. The poor man was probably wondering what he was doing there, and Ben was certain that whatever Elvis' thoughts were, none of it came close to why Ben was truly present.

Neither man said anything. They just stared at each other — one in shock and the other in awe.

Ben sighed. He was going to spare the man the trouble. "Hello, Elvis. I'm-"

"Jesse Stockholm." Elvis finished for him. "I know who you are." Mouth slightly open, he looked at Ben.

Right. What was he thinking? Ben scratched the back of his head and chuckled nervously. He beamed at the man standing in front of him.

He shouldn't be surprised, yet he was. Of course, Elvis knew who he was. He'd be stupid not to. For one, Ben was into the kind of music Elvis vibed to, which led to two. Anyone who listened to his song would recognize him even with the beards, and honestly speaking, regular listener or not, Ben had made a name for himself. He had long ago risen to stardom.

"You're probably wondering why I'm here." Ben cleared his throat. "How about I let you finish what you're doing first, then we can talk? Hmm? How's that?"

Elvis furrowed his brows. "Yeah, uh, sure."

Ben felt bad for catching off guard. Millions of questions were probably running through his mind right now, and the patience to wait till he was done sweeping the popcorns from the floor was most likely thin, but it had to be done. But, first, he needed to discuss with Elvis that he had a clear mind and wouldn't steer towards an unfinished job. Plus, he knew Elvis had to get the place clean for the next movie.

"I'll be waiting outside. Take your time." Ben smiled at Elvis and made his way outside.

That was...

Ben had no words, but he let out a huge sigh of relief once he stepped out. He was a wreck in there. He wasn't sure if

Elvis noticed it, but his hands were shaking when they were talking. *Shit! I didn't even rehearse what I'm going to say to him.* He shook his head in disapproval. *Good going, Stockholm. Good going.*

It didn't take too long before Elvis emerged from the theatre, broom, and packer in hand. Rather than approach Ben, he made his way to one of the doors to empty his hand and came out again. This time Presley approached Stockholm.

There were whispers. People wondered what relationship both men had. But, especially since Ben jumped up happily when Elvis came towards him, he smiled and put his hand around a confused Elvis, leading him outside. If anything Ben knew, those in the theatre weren't as perplexed as Elvis was. He chuckled inwardly.

As they made their way outside, Ben caught his companion stealing glances at him. He shook his head, smiling. "Don't worry; I'll satisfy your curiosity soon."

He stopped dead in his tracks. "Wait! Is it okay that I'm taking you out? Shit. I didn't even if it was. Let's go back. I don't want to get you into trouble." Ben turned back, grabbing Elvis by the shoulder.

"It's okay. You probably didn't notice, but I already told one of my colleagues that I'd be stepping out."

Huh? When did he do that? I was sitting right there, and I didn't notice anyone go in before him. Plus, the door was locked. I saw him unlock it. Or did I miss something? Nah. He scrunched his brows. *I'm sure he was the only one that went in there.*

Ben laughed. "You did, huh?" *My idol just lied to me.* He looked very smug and felt very much accomplished. If the man standing in front of him with a *you-got-me* expression on his face wasn't making a big deal out of it, he wasn't going to press him. Maybe the supervisors weren't so strict with the employees. Or maybe his idol had thrown caution to the wind just for him. He decided to go with the latter. Being famous surely came with certain perks.

The star grinned at his role model. "Well then, shall we?"

✱✱✱

Elvis was smart enough to lead them to a quiet restaurant. Ben had made it clear to him that he wasn't familiar with the area. So, Elvis had to find a place for them. Thankfully, it wasn't bustling with people. The name was ALL YOU CAN EAT. It looked decent, both ok the outside and inside. Ben found it out as one of Elvis' favorite diners.

Here he was, in a restaurant with the one person he looked up to the most, the one who made him who he was today. Although the other party didn't know that, it felt too surreal. It was a dream come through for Ben Stockholm. One he'd never initially thought possible.

Ben decided to take care of the bills. They both ordered what they wanted and Ben, not wanting to beat around the bush, dived right into the discussion.

"Elvis, I'm going to be straight with you. I've heard you sing. Not once, not twice, but the much I've heard is enough for me to know you've got talent and more potential than you know." He wanted to get this out of the way. If he wasted any time having small talk, he'd become a nervous wreck. It was knowing you had something to do but didn't want to get to it yet, so you had to reward yourself with something so that you could get to it.

Only, this time. He would reward himself after. The small talk would possibly lead to the heart-to-heart talk he so wanted could come later. He'd make certain of it. But, for now, it was strictly business.

The other man looked at him. Something akin to a frown and confusion was evident on his face. However, he said nothing, waiting for Ben to continue.

"I'd like to manage you."

"Huh?" Elvis' didn't look convinced. "I don't understand. Manage me? Why?" Ben couldn't blame him. The first day they met, they'd only exchanged a few words, and now, he was here talking about managing him. It just didn't add up.

Ben didn't know how else to explain. He could only hope Elvis would reason with him. Only, being reasonable wasn't an option if he didn't give the other man a better explanation and why.

"I need you to trust me, please. I know how much you love music. I asked around, plus I've heard you sing— a couple of

The King & Elvis

times at most. It was enough to convince me. I've reached a point in my life where I think that rather than continue to be in the spotlight, I wouldn't mind being the catalyst to getting someone else there. And I'd be happier knowing I have a hand when things turn out great.

"So please, let me do. I want to get you there. To stardom. You and me together. What do you say, Elvis?" All the while Ben had been speaking, he had his fingers crossed under the table, hoping to the universe that he wouldn't get turned down. If someone was going to get Elvis there, he wanted to be the one. He somewhat felt he owed him that much.

"It's not that I didn't want to. Heck, I'd take up the first opportunity I got to do something like this. It was just too sudden, that's all. And for whatever reason, thank you for choosing me. I guess I owe it all those you asked around, hmm?" Ben simply grinned. "No, Elvis. It's all you."

Satisfied with the way things had turned out. Ben leaned back on his seat. He took a bite of the hotdog on his plate. "I'll need to know your schedule. That way, I'll know how to fix you up at the studio."

Agreeing meant a lot of sacrifices, not just on the part of Elvis but Ben. First, he needed to come up with the perfect time to fix Elvis. To fit him in his schedule somehow, but that was something he could figure out. So now, they drink and just talk.

✳✳✳

Together, Elvis and Ben made history. The two men created some of the most soul-touching songs. They made songs that people danced to and those that made people look deep into themselves. Likewise, Presley and Stockholm were deep in their elements together. They complimented each other, and where one lacked, the other made up for.

What people loved the most was that they were able to channel their voices to different sides. Their versatility was something to look out for, from groovy to soul touching to both. Everyone loved them. They were an unstoppable force in the industry — one to reckon with. And soon, they went global.

Ben always made sure Elvis was around whenever he had practice with the band. They'd all gotten used to having him around. Sam too. Since the Taking Care of Business band members, Elvis was the first person Ben had brought in in a while.

Ben had initially informed him about Presley, and being that Sam trusted his hindsight, speedily agreed. The star told him of his plans to manage him personally, and Sam didn't oppose. On the contrary, he was proud of Ben's decision, and he looked forward to the kind of man Elvis would turn out to be.

Of course, Sam had told him he was readily available should he need his advice on anything. At first, Sam had been the one managing Ben, but after the band members came along, Sam knew being both producer and manager wouldn't be an easy task. Especially since the number of people he would manage had increased in number. Someone else had been in charge, but Sam was still behind it all.

With all hands on deck — each performing their duties, Jesse Ben Stockholm, Elvis Aaron Presley, the Taking Care of

Business band, Sam Phillips, the Sun Records. All employees of the record label soared higher than they ever bargained for.

Everyone was happy. And not just Memphis, but everyone else around the globe who was familiar with what they could do.

CHAPTER 13

Jesse Ben Stockholm was slowly nearing a storm he could never go back from — old age.

The man was past his youth, and now he was old enough. Old enough to have bigger responsibilities. A wife. Child. A family.

So much time had passed. And Ben's name had become a sensational one. Though a lot of people stilled called him Jesse, he felt more like Ben than Jesse.

In the long run, he and Elvis had become inseparable, along with the Taking Care of Business band members.

Ben had managed Elvis quite thoroughly, and Elvis saw him as more than just a manager. Ben became a friend, a brother, and a mentor to Elvis. Sometimes it all seemed too unreal to Ben, but either way, he'd already gotten used to it. Elvis had even started calling him Ben. He said to Ben once that it made him feel closer to him.

Ben noticed only his close friends and colleagues from the army called him by his middle name. In a way, Elvis was right. He felt closer to those who called him Ben than those who called him Jesse. Some of his fans referred to him as Ben sometimes, but a vast majority stuck to Jesse Stockholm.

Of course, there was Dorothy. His first love after his mother. Like he'd suspected, Dorothy had built a place in his heart. He still loved her, and there were days he longed for her, but at last, he eventually came to terms with the fact that she was never coming back. Of course, he missed her, but he never let his memories of her get in the way of other relationships he had.

After Dorothy, Ben had a series of other relationships, but neither of them ever really lasted. Some he dated, some he got into something serious with but very few could hold his attention for so long. Which was why when he met his next love, something clicked. And it was so serious that Ben was ready to settle down finally.

With Olivia, Ben saw a future with her in it. And slowly, he finally let go of his old flame, Dolly. She became old news with Olivia now in the picture. Although his dead ex-lover had a space in his heart, not like they had bad blood before her death, Olivia completed Ben in many ways that he thought possible. This was one reason why when he found out she was pregnant, Stockholm immediately wanted to do things the right way.

He proposed to her the next day. And she said yes! Ben had never been happier. Together, the couple was happy. They understood each other.

Where Ben was impatient, Olivia was rational and a no-nonsense woman. Though kind and sweet, she was a disciplined woman. She knew exactly how to put Ben in his place should he misbehave. Just like the judiciary carries out checks and balances exist, Olivia not only existed as his lover and partner but also to put Ben in check. His friends didn't think anyone could do a better job than she. Ben thought so too, and he was grateful to her for it.

Stockholm did so much, and not just for himself but those around him. It was almost impossible not to love him. For example, Elvis. Normally, he would have died from a drug overdose, but Ben could prevent that by making sure he didn't go the wrong way.

Ben learned some life lessons himself, and time passed. Like, finally being able to stay true to himself and never make another man your idol— a lesson he also taught his son, Liam. He'd named him after his father. Of course, someone who knew his story wouldn't expect it, but that was the case. Though he never liked to admit it, he missed his father dearly. Memories of his childhood might have been gone, but he was still his father.

He knew he wouldn't be here without him. And his mother? How dearly he missed her. The singer longed to see hear her sing again, but he knew it would take more wishful thinking for that to happen. He even consoled himself with the fact that he might live long enough to witness the birth of his parents.

However, where would he start from? Of course, he'd have to find his grandparents first, then watch them closely, but that wasn't even an option. Rather than chase after the future that was in the past, he resolved to focus on the now and enjoy it. He was going to make the best of all that was in front of him.

***

Time flew by. Ben had long become a family man. He had not just a wife to cater for but a son too. His sweet, sweet boy, Liam Junior Stockholm. Liam Jnr had his grandfather's eyes, from who Ben had also inherited the feature. But, unlike his father, Ben Stockholm vowed to be there for his son, to always be present in his life no matter how work tried to take him away. He promised to put family first before anyone or anything else. And he did.

Although the star vowed to focus on the present, he still went by living each day to meet his parents one day. There was so much he wanted to do and say.

If there was one person he remembered vividly from his time in the year 2040, it was Elias Abendroth. Somehow, he couldn't seem to forget him. There were days Ben would think about him. He wondered how the man was doing and if he ever felt responsible for him leaving. After all, he could have said no. Ben remembered when he tried to talk him out of leaving.

Maybe I should have stayed. I probably should have listened. I had my life in front of him, and I gave it all up for what? A man? But then I wouldn't have Liam if I didn't leave. He suspected he could have amounted to someone great had he stayed behind. Maybe not as great as now, but how bad could it have been? He remembered the silent words that echoed when he called his mother before he left. Am I not enough? Is this reality not enough?

Ben suspected his mother blamed herself for him leaving. Lisa Reed probably felt she should never have introduced Elvis to him. But until how long until he would have discovered the singer himself. Or maybe not.

Back in the beginning, when he first arrived in Memphis. Ben had left home with the hope that Elias Abendroth would find a way to bring him back. Thinking back, Ben tried to imagine how possible it would have been. Would the scientist have tried to find him? Even so, where would he start to look for him from?

So many unanswered questions, and it's not like he would ever be able to find the answer to them. So why bother? Ben sighed. He rubbed the middle of his temple. "All this thinking won't help me. What's done is done. I can't go back, nor can I bring my parents here. I can't turn back the hands of time. I already messed with it, and I might as well stick to it."

Ben Stockholm had altered history big time. From using the time machine down to Gladys Presley and Elvis Presley. His presence in this time alone was a big enough alter. The people he met, and the one he married and gave birth to. He couldn't help but think, however, if all of it was meant to be. Maybe there isn't anything for me there but here. Maybe I was born to do this. Or maybe not… what was the use if the history had already been made. He was just at the wrong time.

The cool breeze of the night hit him. Among the many things Ben enjoyed about the countryside was the open field. But, of course, being rich came with its perks, one of them the gigantic plot of land he bought.

At the initial stage, he wasn't sure where he'd wanted to settle down. There in the countryside or somewhere across. A different state, maybe. It wasn't he'd spoken to Olivia about it, did they decide. But, in truth, he didn't mind where it was. He knew he'd be able to adapt quickly, whichever way.

Olivia had been the one who chose Texas. His wife loved the countryside so much, but at the same time, she didn't want to be stuck in Memphis her whole life. So she chose Travaasa Austin, Texas.

Still busy with his thoughts, he heard shuffling. Ben turned to see what it was; he smiled when he saw the figure approaching him.

"What are you doing up late, Liam? Shouldn't you be in bed?" He scooped the little boy in his arms. Liam just turned two years a while back. He was growing fast. Unlike kids his age, Liam was already reading storybooks. So many of them were science. His little boy seemed to be fascinated by space.

When he'd first noticed, he was scared because he thought his son would be the one to pay for his actions. But gradually, Ben had accepted it. Rather than let him stray from the right path, Ben vowed to guide his son like his father. In the end, should something like what happened with him, he would take it. He'd made Lisa and Liam worry after all; what's to say his child won't do the same?

The little boy squirmed in his father's eyes. He looked sleepy. "Mommy is getting me water." Little Liam rubbed his sleepy eyes, trying to stay awake. "I came to see the stars, daddy."

Ben chuckled. "The stars, huh?" He ruffled his son's hair playfully. "You're lucky it's a Friday, young one. You know I wouldn't let you stay up if it wasn't." Liam spared his father a cheeky grin—showing off some of his missing teeth.

"Hey, I heard someone magical is coming tonight." Liam looked at his dad, smiling. "The tooth fairy?" Ben feigned shock. "What! Did she already stop by? Did she make sure to leave your tooth under the pillow, hmm?"

Liam giggled. His tiny hands were gripping his father's shirt. "Daddy! There's no tooth fairy."

Ben gasped, playing along. He silenced his son with an index. "Sshhhh. Don't let her hear you, or you'll be sorry. She's real son, and she once came for my teeth." He pointed at one of his incisors. Look here, this one, it was when she came to collect this I saw her. And you know what she did when she caught me peeking?"

His son was no longer laughing as he listened to his father closely. He shook his head.

"This!" He reached for the young child's sides, tickling him playfully. Once again, Liam giggled. He wiggled in his father's arms, trying to break free. His laughter was getting louder by the time. "Da- dad-daddy."

Olivia had joined them. She dropped the cup of water by the water and folded her arms. She looked at her husband and child in admiration. Nothing but pure love written on her face. She let them have their moment for a bit before she started. "Ben." Had voice was soft. She smiled, her arms open in expectation. He ruffled his hair one last time before giving his son to his mother.

"You'll need some water after all that laughing," Olivia said to her son as she scooped him up in her arms. She grabbed his cheek playfully and judged her nose against his. Ben took the water and had it to her. "Drink, sweetie." Liam grabbed the cup, helping himself.

His parents smiled. Olivia shared a knowing look with her husband. How independent. Unless he felt the need for it, he rarely let anyone help him do anything. And they never complained. They'd made a promise to help him all the way, but they both never wanted to force their child to anything.

It sometimes made Ben wonder if Olivia was truly from this time. Certain things she did, women at that time didn't. She was never one to force anything on someone, and she wasn't about to start with her child.

He'd witnessed it a lot of times. Women reprimanded her for her behavior. They'd warned her not to go easy on him as he was still a child. But, of course, Olivia being Olivia, would tell them to mind their business and focus on their own family and leave hers alone. She didn't care for the sentiments of those around her. "Different strokes for different folks," she would say. "Tend to your child and leave mine be."

It was another thing he loved about his wife, amongst the many others he discovered each day.

It felt as though time stopped for a while. Ben stood, looking at the two people in front of him. He loved his wife and son so much. More than anyone in the world. The day he'd become a father, he'd sworn to be there for him and his darling wife, Liv.

Liam looked sleepy, he noticed. "Liv, let's go inside. He looks sleepy as it is." He kissed his wife on the cheek and Liam on the forehead. He let them go in before him. "Go first, and I'll be right behind you. Need to shut the doors." His wife nodded, handing him a cup.

***

Ben had finally reached a fruitful age. He lived to old age, forever known as the king of rock and roll—Jesse Stockholm. He was both Jesse and Ben. The idol and the person. A role model and a father. If there was anything to be grateful for, it was that he had indeed found and accepted his true self.

He'd gotten to a point in his life where he chose not to regret his actions and live as it is. Rather than ponder on the past, he basked at the moment. He made sure to do his best in everything he found himself doing. He'd received many awards. He'd lived life—a good one.

He was happy. He no longer had regrets.

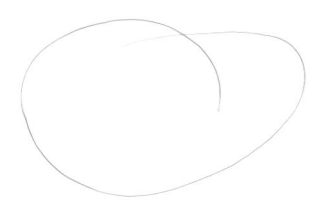

Printed in Great Britain
by Amazon